Fate is a Sweet Lady

C S Farabee

Farabee Publishing
Arizona

This book is a work of fiction. Names, Characters, places, and incidents either are the product of the author's imagination or are used fictitiously, and any resemblance to actual persons living or dead, business establishments, events or locals is entirely coincidental.

Farabee Publishing
Chandler, AZ 85224
www.Farabeepublishing.com

ISBN: 9781942526186
Library of Congress Control Number: 2014922084

Printed in the United States of America

Book Cover designed by: David Mor

We have to believe there is a time for everyone.
A time when we have an encounter that will change our life.
Is it a matter of Fate?

To everyone that believes in Fate and for those that need
more convincing.

Tempting Fate

Marian was finally going on vacation. She usually made reservations to go out of town every two months for a long weekend, but this year was too fast paced. She just could not get away. As she drove her SUV to her cabin, she looked at the snow that was gathering on the side of the road.

She smiled as she thought about that time, years ago, when she purchased the land, and how hard she worked until she had her cabin built. There was no need to work as hard as she does, her books were selling well, she had obtained the status she sought in the academic world and was called on constantly as an advisor and speaker.

She sighed and wondered why she didn't feel complete? Why did she still drive herself as she did? What was missing? She had planned it out, achieved every goal and should feel successful, accomplished, but she still felt like she had to achieve more.

The little town, located a few miles from her cabin, came into view. She pulled into the empty parking lot of the little grocery store and reached for the grocery list she had prepared for her three-week stay. Was she doing the right thing, coming up here for the holidays instead of staying close to her family? She shook her head and got out of the SUV. Why was she questioning herself? It just showed how tired she was. Mrs. Meghan was behind the counter when she entered the store.

"Ms. Carstairs, what a lovely surprise. Merry Christmas."

Mrs. Meghan was a tall woman in her late sixties. She always had a smile for everyone. "Hello Mrs. Meghan and Merry Christmas to you. I'll be staying for a few weeks and need some supplies."

Mrs. Meghan looked like she was going to say something but only smiled and said, "Well, be careful up there all by yourself. There's a storm coming in and I don't believe you've been up here during this time of year before. Two years ago we were snowed in for several weeks."

Marian nodded and started gathering her supplies. Mrs. Meghan watched Marian for only a moment before she busied herself behind the counter. She had never seen Marian bring anyone with her to her cabin. For some reason, that always bothered her. She also noticed that she was not her usual happy self this trip. "I purchased another one of your books. Will you autograph it for me?"

Marian paused from gathering her supplies and turned to Mrs. Meghan. "Of course. How did you like it?"

Mrs. Meghan smiled, "I loved it. You write the most wonderful books. They all have a happy ending."

Marian stared at Mrs. Meghan for a moment before walking towards her and opened her latest book to sign it. 'Happy endings.' Was that what was missing in her life? A happy ending?

Marian signed the book then went back to gathering her supplies. She brought them to the counter and as soon as they were purchased she gathered several bags and headed towards the door. The door opened before she reached it. She stopped and stared at the man that entered. He was tall, looked like he was in his late forties and used two canes to walk.

Brian Mason moved slowly through the door and stared at the woman blocking his path. He knew he should move aside but was spellbound and he didn't know why. He couldn't put an age to her but she looked to be at least in her late forties.

Mrs. Meghan watched as Marian and Brian stared at each other and felt hope in her heart. If anyone needed someone, it was these two. She cleared her throat and moved towards them. "May I help you Mr. Mason?"

Brian looked at Mrs. Meghan and moved aside, allowing the woman to exit the store. "Yes, Mrs. Meghan. I'll need some things for a few weeks."

Mrs. Meghan took the grocery list handed to her and began gathering his supplies.

Marian moved to her SUV and opened the back door to put her groceries on the seat. She did not know what had just happened. She never did that before. There was something about Mr. Mason that caught her. 'Caught her?' Marian shook her head and was returning to the store when a tour bus pulled up. Dozens of people got out and went into the store.

Marian automatically thought of Mrs. Meghan being alone and trying to help all these people. She entered the store and found what she thought she was going to see. Mrs. Meghan was swamped with questions while trying to run the counter. Mr. Mason had stepped aside and was looking at all the people in surprise.

Marian moved towards Mrs. Meghan and took her by the arm. "You get behind the counter and I'll take care of the rest."

Mrs. Meghan looked grateful as she moved behind the counter to ring up everyone's purchases. "Thank you Ms. Carstairs."

Brian watched Ms. Carstairs talk to the customers and direct them to what they wanted. She answered questions about the area and an hour later, the people on the tour were all on the bus and going on to the next stop. Mrs. Meghan and Marian both laughed after the last customer left.

"I didn't know you had tours during winter also," Marian said.

"Not very many but we do get a few. Thank you for your help."

Marian shook her head. "It was my pleasure."

Brian was silent the whole time the store was in chaos and watched as Mrs. Meghan and Ms. Carstairs worked as a team to manage the customers.

They both turned to him at the same time. Mrs. Meghan said, "I'll finish your list for you now Mr. Mason."

Marian looked at Mr. Mason for only a moment before she gathered the rest of her supplies and took them out to her SUV. She returned to tell Mrs. Meghan good-bye and saw the amount of groceries Mr. Mason had purchased. "Mr. Mason, May I help you put your supplies in your car?"

Brian was going to say no. But the usual anger he felt when someone tried to do something for him didn't surface, so he nodded instead. Maybe it was because she asked.

Marian smiled and began taking bags of groceries to his SUV. Brian picked up a few of the bags, balanced them with his canes and followed her to the door. Marian held the door open and watched as he went down the two steps balancing the bags and his canes but didn't offer to help him. He was doing just fine on his own.

She followed behind him with the rest of the supplies and said, "Well, I hope you have a nice stay."

Marian drove to her cabin, brought her supplies in, and was putting them away when she thought of Mr. Mason. He would have to carry all those bags into his cabin by himself. She wondered if he needed help.

Marian didn't give it much more thought. She drove back to Mrs. Meghan's store. Mrs. Meghan knew him so maybe she knew where his cabin was located.

Mrs. Meghan smiled when Marian entered the store. "Did you forget something?"

Marian nodded, "Yes, but not supplies. Do you know where Mr. Mason's cabin is? I thought he may need some help taking the bags in from his car."

Mrs. Meghan nodded and said, "His cabin is two miles past yours. It's at the end of Monroe Lane."

Marian thanked Mrs. Meghan and left. She didn't understand what she was doing. If Mr. Mason needed help, he should have asked.

But here she was driving down Monroe Lane towards his cabin and didn't know why except that he may need help. He would probably send her packing but at least she had made the offer.

Brian pulled up in front of his cabin and looked at the bags in the back seat. There were only two steps up to his front door but it seemed like miles when you have to use two canes to walk. He sighed and got out of his SUV. He opened the back door, grabbed a bag, and started walking towards the front door. He made it to the door and a sharp pain went from his lower back down his right leg. He put the bag down and leaned his head against the door for a moment until the pain subsided. He must be crazy coming up here alone in his current condition. His doctors told him not to go but he had to get away. This past year had been hard and he needed some time away from everyone. He just didn't plan the trip very well.

He sat on the swing on the front porch and waited for the pain to go away completely before he tried to bring in another bag.

He was just getting up from the swing when an SUV pulled up next to his. The woman, Ms. Carstairs, from the store, got out and walked to the steps.

"Mr. Mason. I would like to apologize for not thinking of this sooner, but may I help you with your supplies?"

Brian stared at the woman and again waited for the anger he felt when anyone offered to do something for him but it did not come. Instead, he just nodded and watched her walk to his SUV. He got up from the swing and opened the cabin door for her. She thanked him as she placed the bags on the counter in his kitchen. Brian busied himself with putting away the supplies while she went back out to get the rest of the bags. Marian brought in the last bag and placed it on the counter.

"Well, that's the last of it."

Brian turned to her and said, "Thanks."

Marian noticed how tired he looked but only nodded. "You're welcome Mr. Mason. I'll be going now. If I may be of assistance to you while you're here, please let me know. My cabin is only a few miles from yours."

Brian only nodded and watched her leave. He knew he should have said more but nothing came out. She had said it all.

Marian arrived back at her cabin and checked the woodshed. With a storm coming, she wanted to make sure there was a good supply for the fireplace. It was the only source of heat for the cabin.

She thought of Mr. Mason for only a moment before she opened the shed door and found an abundant amount of wood.

Later that night when she was listening to the radio the newscaster mentioned the storm coming their way and encouraged everyone, that was staying in the area, to make sure they had plenty of wood for heat. It looked like a bad one; possibly even worse than the one they had a few years ago.

Giving Fate A Helping Hand

The next morning Marian could not stand it any longer. After fixing breakfast she drove to Mr. Mason's cabin.

Brian was sitting on the couch in front of the fireplace looking at the wood stacked in the corner. He had heard the weather report the night before. He was going to have to check the woodshed and bring in more wood. He was getting up from the couch when he heard a car pull up in front of his cabin. He frowned and walked to the door.

He opened it as Marian was about to knock. "Oh, Mr. Mason. Good morning. I heard the weather report last night and we seem to have a storm coming. I was going into Mrs. Meghan's to see if there was any more wood available and I wanted to check and see if you had a good supply. Maybe we could go in together."

Brian stared at her again in awe. She had again defused any anger he would have felt of someone checking up on him. "I was just thinking of checking the shed myself."

"Great. Let's see what you have." Marian said as she moved away from the door and started walking towards the shed. "Mrs. Meghan said two years ago everyone was snowed in for a few weeks."

Brian followed Ms. Carstairs slowly. She was standing beside the door of the woodshed when he arrived, waiting for him to open it. He did not understand it but it gave him a sense of strength because she waited for him. She did not see him as an invalid.

Brain opened the woodshed door and walked inside. Marian followed. They looked at his wood supply and neither one was happy. It was only half of what it should be. He would need more.

"Well, it looks like more wood is needed. Would you care to join me on a trip to Mrs. Meghan's?"

Brian nodded and left the shed. Marian waited until he locked it before following him back to the steps. Brian turned to Ms. Carstairs and said, "I'll only be a moment."

Marian nodded and went to stand by her SUV. She pulled her coat closer around her as she waited. It was getting colder already. She looked at the sky but it was still clear.

Brain put his coat on and went back outside. He locked his cabin door and walked slowly down the steps.

Marian moved to stand by the passenger door of Brian's SUV as he moved to the driver's side and got in. He unlocked the passenger door and watched her get in and fasten her seatbelt. He smiled for a moment. There was no question that he would drive. Why did this woman make him feel so strong when she helped him with things? Neither spoke while they drove to Mrs. Meghan's store. When they arrived they were not pleased with what they found.

"I'm sorry but all the firewood has been bought up. I have some logs left that need to be cut. No one wanted them. If you have an axe you could cut it up into firewood."

Marian did not say anything and waited for Mr. Mason to answer. She had plenty of wood but would not offer to share unless it was needed.

Brian looked at the logs and nodded. "Well, I haven't cut logs in a long time but if that is what we need to do let's get it in the SUV."

Marian smiled at Mrs. Meghan and they loaded as many logs as they could into the back of Mr. Mason's SUV. Brian watched as they loaded the logs. Well, they would load the logs and he would cut them up into firewood. It seemed like a fair exchange.

After the logs were loaded, Marian got into the passenger seat and fastened her seatbelt. Brian got into the driver's seat and started the SUV. He looked at Ms. Carstairs for a moment before driving back to his cabin.

Marian wondered if he had a hatchet or an axe to cut the wood but dismissed it because he knew he needed one. She had an axe at her cabin if he did not have one.

Brian parked his SUV next to the shed. They both got out and Marian opened the back of the SUV and looked at the logs. It would take some time to bring them all in. She looked at Mr. Mason who was already walking to the shed and unlocking the door. She took a deep breath, grabbed a log, and walked towards the shed.

Brian found the axe on the wall and tested the edge. Dull. He looked around and found the sharpening stone. He sat down on a chair in the corner of the shed and started sharpening the edge. Marian stopped only for a moment to watch him sharpening the axe.

Brian looked up and said, "Just put the logs outside the shed. There's an old tree stump I have used to break down the logs into firewood."

Marian nodded and went back outside the shed and found the tree stump nearby. She put the log near the stump and went back to the car to get the rest.

Brian finished sharpening the axe and went outside. He picked up one of the logs and placed it on the stump. He took a deep breath, moved back away from the log, and let the axe fall. It hit the log but the log did not splinter. Marian watched but did not say or do anything. This was his part.

The axe was stuck in the end of the log. Brian picked up the axe and levered it again, hard on the tree stump.

The log split. Brian smiled and looked at Marian. She smiled back. Brian split the log two more times and as the pieces fell, Marian picked them up and put them in the shed. After an hour of cutting wood and stacking it Marian said, "Let's take a break."

Brian nodded and sat on the tree stump. He was surprised at how good he felt. His back and legs were not hurting. Sore maybe, but there was no pain like before.

Marian watched him for a moment before she asked, "Mr. Mason, it's cold and I would love a cup of coffee. Do you mind if I fix some for us?"

Brian looked at Ms. Carstairs said, "Brian. And yes thanks."

Marian smiled and said, "Marian. And you're welcome."

Brian watched Marian walk into his cabin and wondered again, what had just happened? She was going to fix them some coffee in his cabin and he did not mind. He shook his head and reached for the axe. The sooner he finished the sooner he could rest.

Marian returned shortly with two cups of coffee and walked towards Brian. She waited until he was through with the log before handing him his cup. Brian accepted the cup and nodded. He sat on the tree stump and sipped the warm liquid. It did not occur to him until he drank half a cup that he did not tell her how he liked his coffee; and yet it was just the way he liked it.

He was going to ask how she knew but stopped when he saw her put down her cup and start gathering the firewood around the tree stump. He finished his coffee and started cutting logs again.

It was some time later when Marian spoke again. "Brian, it's been a long time since breakfast and you've cut a lot of wood. Can I fix you a sandwich or something?"

Brian nodded and kept on cutting the logs. He was almost finished. There were only four more logs to cut.

Marian fixed some sandwiches, brought them outside, and set them on the little table on the porch next to the swing. She waited until he spilt the log on the block and was reaching for another before she said, "Lunch is ready."

Brian looked up and smiled. He reached for his canes and walked to the porch. He climbed the two steps and sat on the swing.

Marian sat on the chair on the other side of the table, handed Brian a rag to wipe his hands and reached for a sandwich.

Brian wiped his hands on the rag Marian had given him and picked up a sandwich.

He had taken several bites before he realized she had done it again. She knew exactly what he liked in a sandwich. He smiled and finished the sandwich and reached for another. You just did not question some things. Besides, after today he would probably never see her again. For some reason this bothered him, but he shook it off. He did not need complications right now.

Marian ate in silence looking out at the scenery. It was beautiful up here. She should make it a point to come here more often. Her mind started drifting to what she would do the coming New Year. She knew she would take more vacations; come to the cabin more often. She looked up at the sky and frowned. When did those clouds move in?

Brian frowned when he saw Marian looking at the sky. "What's wrong?"

"Those clouds are moving in fast. We better finish up and make sure there's enough wood by your fireplace before I leave."

Brian nodded and walked over to the tree stump to cut the last three logs. Marian gathered the dishes and took them back inside to wash them. She looked at his stack of wood near the fireplace and realized it was not going to be enough. She went outside and started bringing in firewood and stacking it in the corner.

Brian saw what she was doing and gathered the splinters he cut from the logs and brought them into the cabin. He was surprised he only had to use one cane.

When the corner was stacked with firewood Marian looked around and smiled. He would be all right now.

"Well, I guess that does it."

Brian frowned and asked, "What about you? We didn't get any wood for your fireplace."

"Oh, I think I may have enough."

Before Brian could remark on her statement, she continued. "Well, I should be going now. I want to get home before the storm hits."

Brian watched her go and thought he should say something. "Marian."

Marian turned to face him. "Yes?"

Brian stared at her for a moment before he said, "Thanks."

Marian nodded, "My pleasure."

Brian watched as Marian drove away and looked up at the sky. It had already started to snow and the winds were picking up. He walked to the tree stump, picked up the axe, and put it back in the shed. When he closed the door, he noticed it was snowing harder and the winds had picked up in just a few minutes. He hoped Marian got home okay.

Fate Lends A Helping Hand

Marian drove down the road to her cabin and started to get concerned. The snow was falling heavy now and the winds had picked up suddenly. She was only a mile from Brian's cabin when she could not see a foot in front of her. She stopped for a minute to get her bearings. The snow had fallen so fast she could not see where the road ended and the woods began. She gripped the steering wheel and drove forward. It was only a short time before a gust of wind pushed her SUV off the road and into a ditch. Her head hit the steering wheel hard and she lost consciousness.

Brian listened to the wind howl outside his cabin and walked to the window. He pulled back the curtain and was surprised at the fierceness of the storm. It had come on so suddenly that he hoped Marian got back to her cabin alright.

Marian woke to a headache and darkness surrounding her. It took her a few minutes to think and focus. She looked around and saw her SUV was half buried in the snow. She rolled down the window and pushed snow away so she could climb out. She pulled her warm winter coat around her as she lay in the snow. It was a good thing she put it on before she started back to her cabin. It was freezing.

The snow and wind were blinding but she sat up slowly. She could not see where the road ended and the woods began. She looked back the way she came and rose to her feet slowly.

The wind was blowing so hard it was pushing her back down. She was exhausted by the time she finally got to her feet.

She knew she could not stay in the SUV but did not know which way to go. She was not sure how far she was from her own cabin.

She looked in the direction she had come and hoped it was not too far back to Brian's cabin. She started to walk against the wind and snow in the direction she hoped would lead her back to Brian's cabin.

Marian walked for a long time before she fell to her knees. She tried to catch her breath but fell on her side. She could not get back up. There was no strength left in her. She lay there freezing and tired. She closed her eyes and asked for help.

Brian became more and more restless in his cabin. He felt Marian needed help. He looked at his canes and cursed them. He looked out the window again and saw that his SUV was half covered in snow. There was no way he could drive anywhere, not in this weather, and his legs were not strong enough for him to walk through the storm to find her. He walked back to the couch, sat down, and stared into the fire. "Please help her."

Marian opened her eyes and sat up slowly. She could not give up. Brian had to be near. The winds slowed and snow fall lightened up a little. She looked around and saw a light in the distance. Brian's cabin. She stood slowly and forced her legs to move through the snow. She just put one foot in front of the other and kept going.

Brian listened to the storm raging outside. Suddenly, it quieted a little. He went to the window and saw the wind and snow had slowed down. He grabbed his coat as he opened his front door. He did not know what he was going to do but he just knew she needed help.

Marian could not walk another step. She fell in the snow and cursed her lack of strength. The light from his cabin was nearer but not close enough. She knew she would never reach it.

Brian stood on the porch for a moment looking out at the snow and thinking about what to do when he stepped off the porch and started walking around his SUV and into the woods.

Something, or someone, was calling to him. It was dark and he could only see where the light of his flashlight shown.

He moved the light around the area in front of him and stopped when it shown on a figure lying in the snow. He rushed as fast as his legs could carry him and knelt down beside Marian. He rolled her over and spoke to her. "Marian! Marian, can you hear me?"

Marian opened her eyes slowly. "Brian. Cold, so cold."

Brian pulled on Marian's arm but she did not respond. "Marian, you have to get up. I can't carry you."

Marian opened her eyes and nodded. She rolled onto her side and sat up slowly. Standing was another matter. She gathered every ounce of strength she had left and rose to her knees, and then stood slowly with Brian's help. He put his arm around her waist and dragged her along beside him. When they reached his cabin, he laid her on the floor in front of the fireplace and started taking off her coat and shoes.

Marian was unconscious as he undressed her. He brought a blanket from the bedroom and a pair of his thermal underwear. He did not think while he undressed her, put the underwear on her and wrapped her in the blanket. He watched her closely and saw color returning to her face and lips. His eyes focused on her lips for only a moment before he went into the kitchen and brought back a cup of hot coffee. He raised her head and gave her some of the hot liquid.

Marian sipped the hot liquid and felt it run down her throat. She opened her eyes and tried to smile but she was too tired. She closed her eyes again and enjoyed the warmth of the fire.

Brian smiled and laid her back down on the rug in front of the fire. He brought another blanket and two pillows from the bedroom. He put one of the pillows under her head, put another log on the fire, and lay down on the couch with the other pillow and blanket. He lay there watching her sleep for a long while before he finally fell asleep.

Brian opened his eyes some time later and looked at Marian. He saw that she had pulled the blanket tighter around her. He put another log on the fire and lay back down on the couch.

The warmth from the fire reached Marian and she snuggled down into the blankets with a smile on her face. Brian smiled and went back to sleep. She would be warm now.

The storm was still raging when Marian woke again. She looked around and saw a pillow and blanket on the couch. She rolled onto her back and looked at the fire. She closed her eyes. She had made it.

Fate Understands You

Brian was in the kitchen when he saw Marian come awake. The coffee was finished brewing and he poured her a cup. "Good morning," he said as he brought the cup of coffee to the living room.

Marian looked at him and smiled. "It is a good morning, isn't it?"

Marian sat up and took the cup of coffee he offered. "Thanks."

Brian went back to the kitchen to get a cup of coffee and was surprised to see that she had followed him. Marian looked down at the thermal underwear she was wearing and smiled. Brian looked at her and laughed. Marian laughed also and sat in a chair at the table. She took a sip of coffee and then frowned. She did not remember anything except the snow and falling down. How did she get to his cabin? "Brian, how did I get here? I don't remember making it to your cabin."

"You didn't. I found you about a hundred yards from the cabin lying in the snow."

Marian looked at him in surprise. "You found me?"

Brian shrugged. "I...I just felt like you needed some help."

Marian smiled. "Well, I'm glad you did. I don't think I would have made it."

Brian nodded and nothing more was said about the strange connection between them last night.

"Do you think you could eat something?" Brain asked to break the silence.

"Yes. I am starved." Marian replied realizing that it was true. She was very hungry.

Brian moved into the kitchen and began taking food from the refrigerator.

Marian watched him and asked, "It may go faster if I help. Is there anything I can do?"

Brian looked at Marian and nodded. "You can cut up the potatoes."

"Great, where is your bathroom and I'll be ready in a minute."

"Down the hall, on your right."

Marian washed her face and combed her hair. She moved too fast at one point and she felt dizzy. She felt the knot on her forehead and slowed her movements. She did not remember hitting her head on the steering wheel until then. She had better take it easy for the rest of the day.

Brian grew concerned. Marian had been gone for a long while. He started towards the bathroom but stopped when she appeared in the hallway.

"Sorry, I felt a little dizzy."

"Maybe you should lie down and let me finish breakfast."

Marian shook her head and put her hand on the wall to steady herself. "No, I can peel potatoes sitting down. I want to help."

Brian stared at her for a moment before turning around and headed back to the kitchen.

Marian walked slowly to the table and sat down. Brian had placed a bowl, knife, and the potatoes on the table for her. She peeled the potatoes and cut them up. Brian took the bowl of potatoes and washed them off before adding them to the frying pan.

Marian sat quietly and watched him cook their breakfast. She noticed that he did not use his canes while in the kitchen. The distances he had to walk were short and he managed nicely.

He would hold onto the counter often to balance himself. She wondered what had happened to cause him to have to use canes to walk but said nothing.

Brian could feel Marian watching him as he fixed their breakfast. He did not feel uncomfortable moving around having to hold onto the counter now and then for balance. It was strange how he felt so comfortable with her.

Marian watched Brian and started feeling dizzy again. She stood, walked slowly to the blanket in front of the fireplace, and lay down. She put her head on the pillow and closed her eyes.

Brian felt Marian leave the kitchen and turned to watch her walk slowly to the blanket in the living room and lie down. He frowned for a moment, turned off the stove and grabbed one of his canes to walk into the living room. He watched her as she lay on the blanket and was wondering what was wrong.

He knelt beside her and put his hand on her arm. "What's wrong Marian?"

Marian opened her eyes slowly and said, "I felt dizzy again sitting at the table."

Brian frowned and sat on the floor next to her. He felt her head and it was cool, no fever. Then he noticed the bump on her forehead just above her hairline. "When did you hit your head?"

"When the SUV went into a ditch my head hit the steering wheel. I lost consciousness for a while."

Brian frowned again. This was not good. She could have a concussion. He had been through enough doctors and examinations to pick up a few things. He had read many books on injuries and trauma's. "Marian, you could have a concussion. I'm going to ask you some questions." Brian paused for a moment before he began the questions.

"Alright." Marian said trying not to smile at how serious Brian sounded.

He held up three fingers. "How many fingers am I holding up?"

Marian smiled at Brian and answered, "Three."

Brian smiled and asked, "What is today's date?"

"December 20th."

Brian nodded. He could not ask when her birth date was because he did not know it and would not know if she got it right or not. "Okay, name as many states as you can."

Marian started naming the states she had visited in the past few years and Brian finally held up his hand. "Okay, that's enough," he said smiling. "I guess you are going to be alright. Just take it easy today and rest."

Marian smiled at him and said, "I'll just lie here and rest while you finish fixing breakfast."

Brian looked towards the kitchen and back to Marian. "I'll call you when it's ready."

Marian nodded and closed her eyes. Her head did not really hurt that much. It was the dizziness that caused her concern. She hoped resting today would take care of the dizziness. She listened to the wind raging outside and knew she would probably not be going home today anyway.

Brian placed breakfast on the table and called for Marian.

Marian opened her eyes at the sound of Brian's voice and looked towards the kitchen. He was standing by the table waiting for her.

Marian sat up slowly and did not feel any dizziness. She rose slowly off the blanket to stand next to the couch and still did not feel dizzy. She smiled and walked slowly to the table. They sat down and began eating. Brian and Marian did not speak until the meal was finished.

Brian asked, "How do you feel? Any dizziness?"

Marian shook her head slightly. "No. I just have a very slight headache."

Brian went to the cupboard to the left of the sink and brought a bottle of Tylenol back to the table. "Take a couple of these."

Marian took a couple of the Tylenol and started to gather the dishes from the table but Brian stopped her with a hand on her arm. Marian looked at his hand on her arm and froze.

Brian removed his hand quickly and said, "I'll take care of the dishes. You need to rest today."

Marian did not argue and went into the living room to lie back down on the blanket on the floor. Brian was going to tell her to move to the other bedroom, but she needed the warmth of the fire.

What he did do though was to remove his blanket and pillow from the couch. "Marian, please let's move you up onto the couch."

Marian sat up slowly and did not argue with Brian. She was so tired she could hardly keep her eyes open.

Brian moved her blanket and pillow to the couch. Marian lay on the couch and Brian covered her with the other blanket. He was concerned when Marian said nothing and as soon as her head hit the pillow she was asleep. Well, he was not a doctor so he would just watch her and get her to a doctor as quickly as possible if need be.

Fate Listens

The morning went fast. Brian brought some work with him and was sitting at the kitchen table working on his laptop. He stopped working when he noticed Marian was sitting up on the couch. He saved what he had been working on and reached for his cane. He did not know why but since yesterday, he only needed one cane for balance when he walked.

Marian sat up and put her head in her hands. She had the most awful headache. It almost brought tears to her eyes.

Brian stopped when he saw Marian holding her head in her hands. He turned around and went back into the kitchen for the Tylenol and a glass of water. He put the bottle of Tylenol in his pocket and carried the glass of water.

When he reached the couch, he sat down beside Marian and held out the glass of water for her. "Here take this. I have some more Tylenol for you."

Marian took the glass of water from Brian and held it with both hands.

Brian noticed this. He took two Tylenol from the bottle, took back the glass of water, and handed her the tablets. Marian put the tablets in her mouth and reached for the glass of water.

Brian could see how unsteady her hands were and helped hold the glass as she drank.

Marian drank all the water in the glass and laid her head back. She never got a headache. She did not understand this.

Brian did not know what to do except take the glass from Marian and return it to the kitchen. He thought of what else he could do and cursed himself for not knowing. She was a kind woman and he wished he could help her.

Marian sat on the couch for a moment trying not to think of anything. Just clear her mind. Maybe it would help. She had been doing too much for too long this year without a break. Maybe that was what was wrong. Being caught in the snowstorm, struggling against the wind, and almost freezing to death must have taken its toll on her.

Brian returned to the couch to sit next to Marian. "Marian, how do you feel?" He put his hand on her forehead and did not feel any fever. "You don't have a fever. That's good. You just need to rest."

Marian nodded slightly and leaned over to lay her head back on the pillow. Brian stood so she could stretch out on the couch.

He covered her with the blanket and put another log on the fire. At least they would be warm.

He went back into the kitchen and looked in the cupboard next to the refrigerator. There were some cookbooks his sister had given him years ago. He kept them at the cabin. He was glad he had them now. Chicken soup was supposed to be good for people who did not feel well. He could make her some chicken soup.

Brian found the recipe and gathered the ingredients. He had been on his own for a long time and learned to cook but he had never made chicken soup.

Marian slept the rest of the afternoon while Brian made the soup and worked on his laptop. He wished he could call someone but there was no service for his cell phone in this area.

Brian listened to the weather report. The storm was not due to pass through until late tomorrow. The roads were closed and would be days before they would be cleared. He checked his food supply and made up a menu so that it would last at least a week. The wind was still too strong to leave the cabin and he wanted to check the generator.

They did not check it yesterday when they looked in the shed. He had enough wood for the fire but he did not know if they had enough fuel for the generator.

Brian found candles and matches. At least they would have light. He looked for the old camp stove he had stored in the pantry and not only found the camp stove but fuel he would need to cook with if the generator went out. He felt better. Now at least they could still cook and have light.

Brian looked around the cabin and made his list of what they would need if the generator went out. He was pleased that they could survive without it. The food supply may be a problem if they were snow bound for more than a week. He had not planned to have a guest.

He looked over at the couch and thought of Marian. He hoped she would be all right.

Brian checked his chicken soup and was satisfied with its progress. He then moved from the kitchen to check the fire and look at Marian. She was asleep and seemed to be resting comfortably. He went back to the kitchen and looked at his laptop. He did not want to work but there was nothing else to do. He did not want to think about the things that were coming into his mind.

He gave up after another half an hour of working and sat staring at this laptop. He had made many mistakes in his life and they would not go away. He sighed and checked on his chicken soup again.

When he returned to the table he opened a new document on his laptop. If he could not stop the memories, he would write them down. Maybe if he got them out of his head they would leave.

Brian spent the rest of the afternoon writing down the memories that bothered him. As he wrote he realized many things.

Everyone makes mistakes but as he was writing about his life he began to see that the decisions he made were based on what he knew at the time and not deliberate mistakes to hurt anyone. He loved his children and at one time, he loved his wife. She had changed after the first few years of their marriage and they drew apart, but they stayed together to raise the children.

He spent more time at work, and she stayed home with the children. When the children left home there was no reason for them to stay together anymore. She filed for divorce and he did not challenge it.

Brian stopped writing and closed his eyes. Clara. Twenty-five years they had been together. They remained friends after the divorce. Two years ago, he was driving her home after a dinner engagement and someone ran a red light. She was killed instantly. He ended up in the hospital with major injuries and two years of operations for him to walk again.

He looked at his canes. Well, almost walk again. He told the doctors he was through with operations and left the city. He needed time alone to think about things. His family and children had been supportive through the past two years but he needed to find where he belonged again.

He looked at what he had written and felt he was getting there. He had been a good husband to Clara, a good provider, a good father to his sons, Mark and Mathew and he was a successful businessman. His brother was running the company and it was doing well. He never had to work again. So why did he feel something was missing?

Thank You Fate

As Marian slept, she dreamed of her life and what she had accomplished. What was driving her? Why did she keep striving to reach a goal she did not understand? Something was missing, but what was it?

Her children were grown and successful, she had her own business and it was doing well, her books were selling, she had succeeded in every goal she had ever set for herself. She was making a difference in the academic field and should feel successful. She had enough money to do whatever she wanted, so why did she feel the need to keep striving for…for what? Where was she headed?

Brian checked on the chicken soup and turned off the stove when he was satisfied it was ready.

Marian woke feeling rested. She looked at the fire for a long while before she sat up and then rose slowly from the couch waiting for the dizziness to begin. She did not feel dizzy and walked slowly to the bathroom.

Brian looked up from his writing when he saw Marian from the corner of his eye. He saw her stand slowly. He wanted to help her but only watched as she made her way down the hallway. He checked his watch and saw that it was a good time to place the bowls on the table and have some soup.

When Marian returned to the living room Brian called to her. "Marian. I made some chicken soup. It's ready if you would like some."

Marian stopped and smiled. "Yes, that sounds wonderful."

Brian smiled and waited until she was sitting at the table before he set the bowl of soup in front of her.

Marian ate the soup and when her bowl was empty, Brian filled it again.

Brian became concerned when Marian only ate the soup and did not say anything. He finally asked, "Marian, do you still have a headache?"

Marian shook her head slowly and continued to eat.

Brian watched her and when she was through he removed her bowl from the table. "Marian, would you like some more Tylenol?"

"Yes, thank you. My head doesn't hurt but I feel…I don't know. Just not myself."

Brian placed two tablets on the table. Marian took the tablets and drank them down with some water.

"Would you like some coffee?"

Marian nodded. "Yes thank you."

Brian watched as Marian left the table, walked into the living room, and sat on the couch.

He cleared the table and cleaned up the kitchen. A cup of coffee sounded good, so he prepared the coffee and brought her a cup, and then returned to the kitchen to pour one for himself.

He sat on the couch next to her and they both sat there in silence and stared into the fire.

Marian broke the silence. "Brian. I want to thank you for everything."

"You're welcome Marian. I'm just glad I found you."

Marian turned to face Brian. "What were you doing out in that storm?"

"Looking for you."

Marian frowned. "How did you know I was trying to get to your cabin?"

Brian shrugged. "I don't know. I just had this overwhelming feeling that I had to go looking for you."

Marian stared at Brian for a moment then shook her head. "Well, strange things happen in this world. Thanks for going out and looking for me."

Brian smiled.

Marian and Brian stared at each other for a long while before Marian turned her head away from him to look back at the fire.

Brian cleared his throat and asked, "I believe there is a deck of cards and some board games in the hall closet. Do you feel like a challenge?"

Marian smiled and looked at Brian. "I haven't played board games or cards in years. What do you have?"

Brian reached for his cane and stood. "Come on, let's see what we have."

Marian followed him to the closet.

"Okay." Brian said as he reached for the deck of cards and handed them to Marian. "Here are the cards." He turned back to the closet and looked at the board games. "We have Monopoly, Sorry, Pay Day, Scrabble and Operation."

Marian looked at the games and thought of all the times she had played them with her children. She did not know if she was up to Monopoly right now, it could take a long time. The rest were okay except she still did not know what happened to Brian but she felt that a game of Operation was not the right choice.

"Let's play a game of cards for a while."

Brian nodded and walked to the kitchen table. "Okay, what do you want to play?"

Marian sat at the table across from Brian. "Well, we could play poker but its better if we had something to play for. I remember when I was teaching my children how to play poker I made the mistake of using jellybeans for poker chips." She laughed then continued. "They kept eating their winnings so I had to change to pennies."

Brian laughed also and remembered teaching his sons to play poker. "I didn't use jellybeans, when teaching my son's to play but we did use beans once."

"I used those a time or to also. Let's play rummy. Do we have a pad and pencil to keep score?"

Brian went to the counter and opened a drawer. He pulled out a pad and a pencil and turned to the table. "Okay. Any special rules?"

"The face cards are ten points and the numbered cards are each five points. The first to reach 500 wins."

Brian agreed and shuffled the cards.

Marian and Brian played cards without talking about anything except the game.

Brian won. He paused for Marian's remark. His wife, Clara, did not like to lose.

Marian sighed and said, "Well, I'll just have to beat you next time. Want to play again?"

Brian smiled and shuffled the cards. "If you feel up to it."

Marian smiled and asked, "If you get me another cup of coffee."

Brian smiled and refilled their coffee cups.

They played another game but this time they talked more. Mostly about their children and the other times they had played cards. Brian did not intend to mention that his wife did not like to lose but it just slipped out. "My wife did not like to lose at anything. So, she didn't play any games with me and the boys."

He looked at Marian for her comment but she surprised him again.

Marian noticed in his comment he used the past tense when referring to his wife. "My ex-husband used to hate to lose at anything. I always loved to play pool and I was good. He would get upset if I won and upset if I lost. I just quit playing after a while."

Brian laid down his cards and said, "Rummy."

Marian frowned and looked at what she still had in her hand. "Darn. That leaves me in the negative for what I have down."

Brian smiled. "Want to play something else?"

Marian shook her head. "No. I'll get you yet."

Brian dealt the cards and Marian won the next hand.

Marian gave a yell when she won. "Rummy. Take that you bully."

Brian looked at what he had laid down and what was left in his hand. He added the numbers and looked at the score. "Well, we are even right now."

Marian smiled. "Okay deal. I am on a role."

Brian dealt the cards and Marian scored 500 before he did.

Brian looked at his watch. "Let's check the weather report again. I made a list of what we have for food and we should be all right for at least a week. My only concern was for the fuel for the generator. We didn't check it yesterday when we looked at the supply of wood for the fire."

Marian frowned, "I forgot all about the generator. Do we have candles?"

"Yes and I also found a camp stove we can use if the generator goes out."

Marian nodded. "Good."

They listened to the weather report together and it did not sound good. There was another storm heading their way after this one let up.

"Well looks like it may be a week or more before we can get you back to your cabin."

"It looks that way. Where are my clothes? I can't wear your thermal underwear all week."

Brian went to the laundry room and brought out her clothes. He had washed them earlier that morning.

Marian smiled and took her clothes. "Where are we going to sleep? I noticed you have two bedrooms but with the fire our only source of heat maybe we should sleep in front of the fireplace."

"The couch opens up to a double bed. We can use that."

Marian nodded. They were both adults it should not be a problem. She had never had any trouble with men staying on their side of the bed so it should not matter where they slept. "Let's open it up and see if we need to put clean sheets on it."

Brian and Marian worked to open the couch into a bed and she followed him to the hall closet for clean sheets. "We have the pillows from the bedroom and also blankets so the sheets are all we need."

Marian took the sheets from Brian and started to make the bed. She put the pillows and blankets on the couch bed and nodded in satisfaction. They should be warm and the mattress was a good one. "Okay. The bed is made." She checked her watch and saw it was too early to go to bed. "What else would you like to do? Want to play a game of scrabble?"

Brian nodded and went to the hall closet. "I used to be pretty good at this."

"Me too. I used to play this every night with my children. After a while, I used to just watch. My daughter and youngest son used to play cutthroat. It was not safe to play with them."

Brian smiled and remembered his sons playing scrabble with him. "My wife would never play but my sons and I used to play for hours. It was the same between the boys. After a while I just refereed their games."

Marian shook her head. "It is amazing what you learn about a person and what they learn playing games isn't it?"

Brian looked at Marian for a moment before answering. "Yes it is."

Marian smiled and went to the kitchen table. "Do you have a dictionary?"

Brian frowned and went back to the hall closet. "No. No dictionary. We'll just have to trust each other."

Marian nodded and opened the game. They each picked one square to see who would go first. Brian won and he again looked at Marian for a response.

"Okay. Let's see what you've got."

And the game began. They talked more as they played. Each put a word down and as they played, they learned a lot about each other.

They learned that each had a good vocabulary, understood how words were used and were conscious of the points they could earn.

Marian won. "Wow. You are good. Let's play with a theme this time."

Brian nodded. "Okay. Pick one."

Marian thought for a moment then said, "How about anything to do with children?"

Brian nodded. "Okay. Since you won you can go first."

They played and laughed. Every time they put down a word, for some reason, they explained why they did. They discovered that each spent a lot of time with their children when they were growing up.

Brian won the game.

Marian laughed when she looked at the words they made and Brian laughed also. He had not felt this good in a long time. He could actually relax around Marian.

"Okay. You pick a theme this time."

Brian thought for a moment then said, "How about types of food."

Marian frowned. "Types of food. That may be hard let's extend that to ways to prepare food also."

Brian nodded and they began. They did the same as before. When they put a word down, they gave an example or explanation of the word.

Marian won the game and yawned. "I'm sorry Brian, but that's all for tonight. I need to get some rest."

Brian put the game away while Marian was in the bathroom. When she came out, he grew nervous. He hadn't slept with a woman for many years. He wondered what she would expect.

Marian came out of the bathroom and went to the sofa bed and lay down then sat up. "I'm sorry. Which side do you want?"

"The left side."

Marian smiled and moved to the other side of the bed.

Brian went into his bedroom to get his pajamas and went into the bathroom. His discomfort of what to say to Marian was wasted time because she had turned her back to him and was sound asleep when he lay down on the sofa bed. He lay there for a long while before he fell asleep.

Fate Is Patient

When he woke in the morning, she was gone. He looked around and saw her in the kitchen. She was wearing her own clothes and fixing coffee. He sat up slowly and reached for his canes, which were leaning next to the couch. He stopped his hand in motion before he reached them. He did not remember putting them both there last night. Marian must have done it.

"Good morning. I fixed you a cup of coffee. Since you cooked yesterday I'll fix breakfast this morning."

Brian looked at Marian. "Sounds good." He went to the bedroom to get some clothes and went into the bathroom. When he came out the coffee was ready and Marian was fixing breakfast. He sat at the kitchen table and asked. "Can I help?"

Marian placed a hot cup of coffee in front of him and said, "It's almost ready. You can fix the toast if you want."

Brian nodded and took several sips of his coffee before going to the counter and put some bread in the toaster.

The storm had passed and it was quiet outside. Marian had turned on the radio after breakfast and they listened to the weather report. The next storm was not due to arrive until late that night. Both wondered the same thing but Brian said it aloud.

"How far is your cabin from here?"

"About two miles. I may be able to make it if the weather holds."

Brian looked out the window and then opened the front door. Snow was piled high against the door. He pushed on the snow with his cane and made a path to walk onto the porch. His SUV was half covered in snow and he looked around the yard.

The shed was half buried in snow and it looked like the rest of the forest surrounding the area was the same. There was no way anyone could walk anywhere in it let alone a couple of miles. "I don't think you'll make it and I can't let you go by yourself."

Marian came up behind him and looked around the yard. "I think you're right. Even if I tried, it would take me all day. Let's look in the shed and see if the generator is going to last."

Brian moved off the porch and made a path with his cane through the snow. When he reached the shed, they both pushed the snow away from the door. When they entered the shed, they could see the generator and plenty of fuel next to it. They both smiled.

"Well, looks like the generator will be okay. Let's hope it doesn't freeze up on us. While we are here and it's calm, let's take some more firewood inside."

Marian nodded and went to pick up a pile of wood. They each made several trips and replenished the stack of firewood next to the fireplace.

Marian followed Brian back to the shed and watched as he refilled the generator with fuel. "How long was the next storm supposed to be in the area?"

Marian thought for a moment. "The weather report said it should only last for a few days then move on."

"The generator may last us then. We have enough firewood and our food supply looks good."

"And we have plenty of games to play."

Brian smiled. When he came up here, he wanted to be alone but now with Marian here he wanted to be with her. He wanted her to stay. He wondered if she felt the same.

"Let's sit on the porch for a while. It's cold but at least we can be outside for a while."

Marian took the broom from the pantry and swept the snow off the porch around the swing and Brian gathered the blankets from the extra bedroom. They sat in the swing and wrapped the blankets around them.

They found comfort in just sitting next to each other. They did not have to talk all the time. Brian really liked that. There were times when he did not want to talk. He just wanted to…be.

Marian liked it that Brian did not always have to talk. She enjoyed just swaying on the swing bundled in the blanket.

They did not know how long they sat there in silence until they saw a rabbit come into the yard. They each watched it for a long while before it disappeared into the forest.

"I wonder how animals do it. They don't have a fireplace to keep them warm or a blanket to snuggle in."

Brian laughed. "They have an extra layer of fat and are bundled in fur."

"Well, the idea of being bundled in fur is appealing but not the extra fat."

Brian laughed and shook his head. "What is it with women and the idea of putting on a little weight?"

"For you men of course. Don't you like how women look in a size 10 and how it fits those curvy bodies? I don't remember ever hearing a man whistle at a woman wearing a size 14."

Brian laughed again. "Don't go blaming us guys. You women do that because you think that is what we want and it's what you want also."

Marian turned towards Brian and asked, "Okay Mr. Man. What exactly do you guys want in a woman? Don't tell me you wouldn't like one of those Hollywood starlets with those perfect bodies and that perfect hair."

Brian put up his hands and said, "Oh no Miss Woman. You are not going to get a word from me on that subject. I like women just fine the way they are."

Marian laughed. "Okay Mr. Man. You are off the hook for now."

Brian thought for a moment then asked, "You know I could turn the tables and ask just what you women want in a man."

Marian looked out across the yard and said, "Well, I'll tell you, but of course, it is off the record."

Brian nodded. "Off the record."

"Well, we women want a man to keep himself in shape. If they expect us to look dazzling and fine then they should be able to see their belt buckle and shoes."

Brian nodded and tried not to laugh but the side of his mouth was twitching.

"Now about character. We women would like a man who is caring and as in tune to our needs as we are to his."

Brian nodded. He would agree with that.

"Also, we would like a man to think of us as a person not only a possession. We do have brains you know and they aren't located below our neck line."

Brian nodded again, thinking it was a good idea to agree even though he was remembering how Marian looked when he was undressing her. It was hard to concentrate on her mind when her body was so well defined.

Marian looked at Brian and asked, "Well what do you think? Is that too much to ask?"

Brian shook his head. "No. And, off the record of course, we men would like a woman to be caring and as in tune to our needs as we are to theirs. Takes care of herself and also remembers that we men have a brain also."

Marian gasped and her eyes grew wide as in surprise of his statement. "Men have a brain also. Well, I never realized that. I suppose I will have to rethink my opinion of men."

Brian laughed. "Didn't I beat you last night in a game of scrabble? You only beat me one of the three games we played."

Marian smiled. "Okay, Mr. Man. I guess you do have some brains. You did come up with some good words."

Brian laughed and looked out across the yard. He stopped laughing and put his arm around Marian's shoulders and turned her toward the yard. "Shhh. Look." He said as he pointed to a deer that peeked its head out of the forest.

Marian looked where he was pointing and smiled. "I haven't seen one this time of year before."

Brian did not remove his arm from around Marian's shoulders for the rest of the time they sat on the porch.

They talked for a long while before they felt it getting colder and moved inside. Brian made lunch and they ate some of his chicken soup and sandwiches.

Marian was going to make the sofa bed back into a couch but thought better of it when she began to get tired after lunch. "Brian, would you mind if I took a nap? I'm starting to feel tired."

Brian shook his head. "No. In fact, I believe I could use a nap also."

Marian smiled and sat on the sofa bed and took her shoes off and lay down. She was asleep in less than a minute.

Brian sat on his side, took his shoes off, and lay down. He lay awake for a while thinking of their discussion on the porch then fell asleep.

Brian woke first and found that Marian had moved over and had laid her arm across his waist. He looked over at her sleeping and put his hand on her arm.

Marian woke when she felt his hand on her arm and stared into his eyes for a moment before pulling on her arm to take it off his waist. "I'm sorry."

Brian held her arm where it was and said, "It's fine where it is."

Marian smiled at him and relaxed. It felt good lying next to him. It had been over six years since she had shared a bed with a man.

Brain smiled back and looked at the ceiling of the cabin. The wind was picking up again and he looked at his watch. "Looks like our storm is coming."

Marian listened to the wind. "Looks like."

Brian removed his hand from Marian's arm, put his arm behind her head, and pulled her towards him so that her head lay on his shoulder. He put his hand on her waist and held her for a long while. Marian closed her eyes and went back to sleep.

Brian pulled the blankets up around them and pulled her closer to him and went back to sleep too. It had been over five years since he had held a woman like this or even wanted to.

When they woke some time later, Brian had moved onto his side. Marian was sleeping on his right arm, and he had his left arm around her waist. She didn't want to move, but Mother Nature was calling. She moved away from him slightly and felt him tighten his hold. "Brian, I have to get up."

Brian opened his eyes and stared into Marian's for a moment before releasing her.

When Marian came out of the bathroom Brian was in the kitchen fixing dinner.

Neither one spoke of the way they slept in each other's arms during dinner nor afterwards when they played another game of scrabble.

Finally, Marian had to say something. "Brian, about this afternoon."

Before she could go on Brian interrupted. "I'd like to apologize for holding you like that. It's been a long time since I slept with a woman and I suppose I just...forgot..."

Marian stared at the scrabble board without answering. There was nothing to say. He had said it all. He forgot. Yes, that was the answer she knew was coming, but had hoped for something different.

Brian watched Marian and knew he had said something wrong. He had apologized but for some reason it did not set right with him. He actually was not sorry at all.

Marian tried to keep her spirits up during the game but it was no use. She just did not understand it. Why were men not interested in her?

Why did he have to apologize for holding her when it felt so right? She shook her head and tried to concentrate on the game.

Brian saw her shake her head and asked, "Is there something wrong?"

Marian placed her word on the board and answered, "No. I was just thinking of a word to use."

Brian knew it was his turn but he was not thinking of a word to use on the board. There was another word he was thinking of and that was 'truth.' "Marian. I..." He swallowed hard and continued. "I liked holding you this afternoon. And when I said I 'forgot' what I meant was that I just forgot that we were only friends."

Marian smiled and said, "I liked holding you too, and we can still be friends."

Brian smiled. He had said the right thing. "I believe when we were talking this afternoon we should have added how important it is to speak the truth to each other."

Marian nodded. "Yes. People's imaginations can run away with them. Let's make a pact as long as we're here to tell the truth."

Brian nodded and said, "Okay. That last word you put down was questionable."

Marian laughed and said, "It's a perfectly good word."

Brian shook his head. "I don't think so. How is it used?"

Marian explained and he smiled. "Okay. I'll accept it."

They finished the game and Brian won.

They moved to the sofa bed and sat with their backs leaning against the back of the couch and talked about when they were young.

After a while Marian asked, "How old are you anyway?"

Brian smiled. He looked younger then he was. "I will be fifty-two next month."

Marian laughed. "A baby."

"A baby? How old are you?"

"On no Mr. Man. You know you are never to ask a woman her age."

"I told you."

"Okay. I will be fifty-five in February."

Brian stared at her. "No way. I have seen older woman and you are not one."

Marian laughed. "Older women? Well, I like that."

Brian did not know what possessed him but he put his arm around her shoulders and pulled her to him and said, "Me too." Just before he kissed her.

Marian kissed him back and put her arm around his neck.

Brian deepened the kiss when he felt her response.

Brian pulled back and smiled. "You sure don't kiss like an older woman."

Marian laughed and kissed him again. "You don't kiss like a baby."

Brian held Marian for a long while before they got ready for bed. He put another log on the fire while Marian was getting ready for bed. When she came out of the bathroom wearing his thermal underwear he thought it never looked that good on him.

Marian lay down on her side of the bed while Brian was in the bathroom and wondered what would happen when he returned. She worried that he would want more than just a kiss now and then. She had never been any good at the rest of it.

Brian wondered when he was getting ready for bed if Marian would let him hold her all night. His wife had complained about his lovemaking and he was not sure he wanted to spoil their friendship with anything more than kissing her and holding her. He also wondered if it was because of the storm and their being snowed in together.

Marian remembered what Brian said about truth and decided to talk to him about her fears and about his wife. He had mentioned her only in the past tense but that did not mean that he was not still married.

Brian remembered the pact they made about telling the truth and decided to tell her about his fears.

Fate Never Felt So Good

Marian watched as Brian approached the bed. "Brian…I think we need to talk."

Brian had always dreaded those words from his wife but with Marian it was different. The fear of a fight or misunderstanding was not necessarily forthcoming. "Yes, I agree. We do need to talk."

Marian waited until he was settled in bed before she asked, "Brian, you mentioned your wife but only in the past tense. Are you still married?"

Brian shook his head. "No. We were divorced for three years before she was killed in an automobile accident. I was taking her home after a dinner engagement and a car ran a red light and hit us. I ended up in the hospital but she was killed instantly."

"Oh, Brian I'm so sorry."

"It has taken two years of operations for me to be able to walk again."

Marian laid her head on his shoulder and put her arm across his waist. She did not say anything. There was nothing to say.

After a while Brian asked, "What about you? You said ex-husband. How long has it been?"

Marian knew what he was asking. "I was divorced a long time ago and raised the kids alone. I tried it again ten years ago but it didn't last three years."

Brian put his hand under Marian's chin and raised her head to look into her face. "Are you telling me that it has been what six or seven years since you have been held like this?"

Marian nodded.

Brian could not understand it. She was a beautiful, caring woman. How can men be so stupid? Then he smiled. It was their loss.

He kissed her softly on the lips and put her head back on his shoulder. Marian did not understand Brian's kiss but closed her eyes and enjoyed being held. Neither spoke anymore but fell asleep holding each other. Whatever came out of their friendship would come and they would talk about it when it was necessary.

When morning came the winds were even stronger then the last storm. Brian woke first and kissed Marian softly before he left the bed.

Marian felt his lips on hers and smiled. What a great way to wake up. She frowned when he left the bed and rolled onto her side away from him and closed her eyes again.

She smiled when he returned and turned her so that he could hold her again. "Good morning." She murmured.

Brian smiled. "Good morning." And kissed the top of her head.

They both lay awake holding each other until Marian had to get up.

Brian released her when she pulled away. He decided it was time to get up and fix some coffee and breakfast.

Brian put another log on the fire and started the coffee maker. When Marian came out of the bathroom wearing only a bath towel, he kissed her when he passed her in the hallway to his bedroom.

While Brian was taking a shower, he thought of how Marian looked in nothing but that bath towel. If he had any doubts about his manhood before, he did not now. He looked down and quickly turned the hot water to cold. He gasped and decided it was not worth it and turned it back to hot. He was getting to old for this.

Marian was fixing breakfast when Brian finally entered the kitchen. Before he could ask Marian said, "Can you peel some potatoes?"

Brian sat at the kitchen table and peeled a few potatoes. He rinsed them and handed the bowl to Marian. He kissed her again before he left the kitchen. He could not help himself. She was just so kissable.

Marian smiled. She was happy. Even if this only lasted a few more days she would take it. This is what she had always wanted. To feel special. To have someone kiss her as Brian kissed her and hold her like he held her.

After breakfast, since the storm was still raging outside, they decided to play another board game. They selected Monopoly this time since they had all day. They stopped for lunch and by dinnertime they had bought up all the properties, placed hotels on them and were both running the bank. All the money in the bank was theirs and they broke every rule. They had a great time.

After dinner they were played out on board games and did not feel like playing cards so they sat on the sofa bed with their backs against the back of the couch sipping coffee, listening to the wind rage on outside and just relaxed.

Brian broke the silence. "You know, there is a game we haven't looked at. I just remembered it. There is a list of questions on each card that you ask everyone and there is no right or wrong answer."

Marian thought for a moment then smiled. "Let's look at it."

Brian searched the hall closet until he found it. It was pushed way in the back behind the other games. He brought it back to the sofa bed and sat down next to Marian. "Okay here we go."

He pulled one of the cards from the stack. Each card had several question on it. "Hmm. How about this one? 'If you could save any animal in the world, which on would you save?'"

Marian thought for a moment and said, "I would save the whales. They're already endangered. What animal would you save?"

Brian thought for a moment. "A dog. We had a dog for a lot of years and it brought my sons a lot of happiness."

Marian chose a card and looked at the questions. "If you could climb the highest mountain, what would you leave at the top?"

Brian thought for a moment then answered, "My ancestor's coat of arms."

Marian smiled and thought of her answer. "I would leave a book."

Brian frowned, "A book? What book?"

Marian nodded. "A collection of Mark Twain's stores."

"Why Mark Twain?"

"Because it has humor, sadness, happiness and success." Marian could see that Brian did not understand. "Brian if anything happened to the rest of the world and that was the only place untouched by destruction, think of what the next generation would have to read."

Brian smiled and said, "You are a teacher."

Marian nodded.

Brian selected a card and read through the questions. "What is your favorite sports team?"

Marian scrunched up her face and said, "Sports? My sons tried to get me interested in their football games so I had to select a team. They showed me a list of football team's helmets and I selected the Washington."

"Why the Washington?"

"Because they had the prettiest helmet."

Brian laughed. Evidently she was not a sports fan.

"I do like baseball, though I haven't selected a specific team I like." Marian added.

"I like the Pittsburgh Steelers. Since I was born there it seemed like the right team."

Marian selected a card. "If you had a choice between a 'night out on the town' and a 'quiet evening at home' which would you chose?"

"A quiet evening at home. I never did like going out too much. My wife was always going to parties and social events." Brian shook his head. "I got out of as many as I could."

"I like a quiet evening at home also. Since I'm in front of people all day and sometimes half the night, when I can just sit at home and listen to the quiet its heaven."

Brian pulled a card from the stack. "If you could visit any country in the world, where would you go?"

"I would like to go to Australia. I can't believe I haven't gone there yet. I travel every year to a different state and I have been to Mexico and Canada but that's as far as I've traveled outside of the US."

"Why Australia?"

"I don't know. I have written several novels about it. You would think that I would go to see if I have the details correct."

"Written novels? You're an author?"

"Yes. I've written five novels and they're doing quite well."

"What kind of novels?"

"Mystery and intrigue. The first one I published was a romance intrigue. The rest are more intrigue and mystery then romance. I have a lot of fade outs instead of details in the lovemaking department."

"I'll have to read one. What's your pen name?"

"M.R. Carstairs."

"I've been to Australia and I've traveled to many countries over the past 20 years or so building my business. But if I could choose one special one it would be Ireland."

"Why Ireland?"

"My family came from there. The name Brian means 'high, noble' and 'the strong,' in Celtic."

"Wow. Marian comes from the old French version of Mary. And Mary means 'star of the sea.'"

"Star of the Sea. I like that."

Marian selected a card and tried to not feel the good feeling it brought her when he said he liked her name. "If you could take a picture of anything in the world, what would you take a picture of?"

"My sons and their families. I have three grandsons."

"I have two granddaughters and a grandson. The girls are 15 and 22 months and my grandson is 8."

"My grandsons are 10, 8 and 5 and another due in February."

"Are they sure it is going to be a boy?"

"Actually, they don't know. We're hoping for a girl though. It would be the first girl born in our family for three generations."

"Wow. The family of Kings."

Brian frowned then laughed. "Yes I suppose Kings wanted sons. But a girl would be nice."

Brian selected a card. "Here's a good one. What would be your ideal date?"

Marian closed her eyes and said, "A romantic dinner for two, dancing and then a walk in the park where we could count the stars."

Brian stared at her for a moment then looked back at the card. What would his ideal date be? The romantic dinner for two he could handle but the dancing and the walk in the park would be another matter. Maybe the walk in the park but not the dancing. "The romantic dinner sounds nice and the walk in the park but I don't think I could do the dancing."

Marian looked at Brian and frowned. "Brian this is supposed to be your ideal date. What would your ideal date be?"

"My ideal date would be you."

Marian opened her mouth then closed it. No one had ever given her such a compliment. She learned over and kissed him softly.

Brian returned her kiss and cleared his throat. "Do you think you could do without the dancing?"

Marian smiled. "How about a slow dance?"

Brian smiled. "I think that could be arranged."

Marian jumped up from the sofa bed and turned on the radio. The song that just ended was a fast one and she hoped a slow one came next. And it did. They were playing 'White Christmas.'"

She held out her hand and Brian frowned. "Now?"

"Now."

Brian stood and automatically reached for his cane then stopped. He carefully took a step towards Marian and pulled her into his arms. They swayed to the music and held each other. "Well, what do you know? I'm dancing."

Marian laughed. "And a very good dancer at that."

Brian kissed her and put her head on his shoulder. He felt comfortable and took a step and then another. He managed to even turn a little and move around the room slowly to the music. He was really dancing.

When the music ended, he laughed and said, "Well, it wasn't a fox trot but I did alright."

Marian laughed and said, "We can do that tomorrow."

Brian shook his head and walked slowly back to the sofa bed. He sat down and closed his eyes. There was no pain anywhere.

Marian grew concerned when Brian closed his eyes. Did he hurt himself? She knelt in front of him and took his hands in hers. "Brian, did you hurt yourself? Was it too much?"

Brian opened his eyes and looked into hers. "No. I was looking for any discomfort or pain and didn't find any. I'm fine."

Marian rose to her feet and said, "Good."

The next song that came on the radio was silent night. Brian stood and asked, "May I have this dance?"

Marian put her arms around his neck and said, "Yes, I'd love to."

Brian danced slowly and felt his way as he moved to the music. As long as he moved slowly he could balance while holding Marian in his arms. When the music ended Marian could see by the look on his face that there was some pain so she told him to stay where he was and handed him his cane.

Brian walked slowly to the sofa bed and sat down.

"Brian, where does it hurt?"

"My lower back."

"Lie down on your stomach and let me massage it for you."

Brian laid down his stomach and let Marian message his lower back. It felt good. The pain was soon gone but he did not tell her to stop.

"Is the pain gone yet?" Marian asked.

"Yes. But please don't stop. It feels great."

Marian smiled and moved her hands up to his shoulders and massaged his whole back. Then she began on his legs. She massaged his thighs, calves, and then his feet.

Brian had had many massages before but never like this one. This was…he did not know how to put it. He just knew this was better. There was something in her hands that said something. Something more than just someone that was giving a person a massage.

Marian enjoyed touching Brian. She had always wanted someone to give her a massage like she was giving him and she wondered if he would give her one. She would probably have to ask him but there was something in the asking that took away from the act. When she was through she moved back on the bed and lay beside him. "Feeling better?"

Brian was so relaxed that he could only nod his head. Marian smiled. She turned off the radio, the light and put another log on the fire. It was time to go to sleep. Brian was still lying on his stomach so she lay down beside him and rolled away turning her back to him and went to sleep.

Fate My Friend

Brian lay on his stomach for a long while then realized he must have fallen asleep because when he woke the lights were out and Marian was asleep. She had turned her back to him and he did not like that. Was she angry that he fell asleep after the massage and not given her one? He closed his mind to his thinking. This was not Clara, this was Marian. She would do for others and not expect anything in return. She was the giver not the taker.

He rolled onto his side, rolled Marian over to face him, and pulled her to him. He smiled when she kissed him on the cheek and put her arm across his waist.

He had been right. She was a giver. He would give her a massage tomorrow night.

Marian woke first the next morning and kissed Brian on the cheek.

Brian opened his eyes and kissed her softly on the lips. "Good morning."

Marian smiled and said, "Good morning to you too."

They lay on the bed holding each other and listened to the wind. It was still blowing pretty strong.

Brian looked at the fireplace, got out of bed to put another log on the fire, and went into the kitchen to fix the coffee.

Marian gathered her clothes and went into the bathroom.

After breakfast, they listened to the weather report on the radio. The report said that the storm would be passing late that evening. It would take several days before the roads were clear for travel.

Each wondered what they would do today. Marian noticed some books on the shelf in the living room and wondered over to look at them.

Brian looked at his laptop and thought of a few things he needed to get done.

Marian selected a mystery and looked at the sofa bed. The chair in the living room didn't look comfortable and began making the sofa bed back into a couch.

Brian watched Marian and wondered what she had in mind. "What are you doing?"

"I'm going to read for a while and I thought sitting on the couch would be more comfortable then the chair."

Brian nodded. "I have some work I need to do."

Marian nodded and sat on the couch and opened the book.

The morning passed with Brian working and Marian reading the mystery novel. She thought of a new story and looked around for a pad and pencil. She remembered the ones they had used while playing cards and went into the kitchen to get them.

Brian looked up from his laptop and only watched her.

Marian returned to the couch and began to write the new story.

Brian turned back to his laptop and realized it was time for lunch. He was going to say something to Marian but he could see she was deep in thought about something she was writing and made a sandwich and took it to her. He placed the sandwich and a drink on the table next to where she was sitting. Marian saw the sandwich and drink out of the corner of her eye and looked at Brian. "Thank you."

Brian nodded and fixed a sandwich for himself and sat back down at the table. He did not even notice that he had not used either of his canes to take the sandwich and drink to Marian until he was sitting at the table again. It shocked him at first then he smiled.

When Marian had finished her sandwich and drink she took the plate and glass to the sink and rinsed them. She turned to Brian, took his plate and glass from the table, and rinsed them off too. Brian did not look up from his laptop; he was too deep in thought. Marian kissed him on the cheek and went back to her writing.

It was time for dinner before they knew it. Marian stopped writing and looked at her watch. She frowned and looked at Brian. He was still working on his laptop. She put down her pad and pen and walked into the kitchen. She kissed Brian on the cheek and went to the counter to make some coffee.

Brian stopped his typing and watched Marian. He had never been able to work like this with Clara around. She demanded attention constantly. He wondered what she had been writing. "What were you writing all afternoon? I thought you were going to read a mystery novel."

"I was but then I got an idea for another book. What are you working on?"

"My brother has taken over my business these past two years, but I need to do something now that I am able. So, I've been looking into different marketing ideas for the company."

"What does your company do?"

"We do computer systems analysts. We create new computer systems and improve existing technology and business processes. We are sometimes called software quality assurance analysts when we perform extensive tests on new products."

"Sounds interesting. Have you done much with e-learning or web site design?"

Brian smiled. "Now how did you know that?"

Marian shrugged her shoulders. "I'm a professor of IT and Management. There's a lot going on out there in e-learning and web site design and development."

Brian saved what he had been working on and closed his laptop. "Maybe we need to hire you as a consultant."

Marian laughed. "Don't you dare, I don't have time now for everything I do."

Brian smiled and looked at the time. "Is it really that late?"

Marian nodded and opened the refrigerator. "Whose turn is it to fix dinner?"

"Yours, since you have your head in the refrigerator."

Marian laughed and began putting things on the counter. She had pulled out some steaks from the freezer earlier and put them in the refrigerator. "Well, if I must."

Marian looked in the pantry and saw the ingredients she needed to make Christmas cookies. "Brian, after dinner let's make some cookies."

Brian frowned, "Cookies? Marian I eat cookies. I do not make them."

Marian laughed. "Well, if you want to eat any of these cookies you are going to help make them."

Brian opened his mouth to make a comment then closed it. "I warn you Marian, I have never baked a cookie in my life. Are you sure you want me to help?"

Marian nodded. "It's easy and I'll be there with you."

Brian smiled at the thought of Marian being with him anytime day or night. He turned away from her and frowned. Was he falling in love with her? He shook his head. No, it was just being caught together in the storm.

After dinner, Marian cleaned the kitchen and brought out the ingredients needed for baking the cookies. Brian looked at the flour, sugar, and everything else on the counter and frowned. "You know, if we're snowed in here for a long while, we may need these things."

"I already checked the amounts of what we have. We have plenty of what we need for more than a week. Don't forget I have plenty of food at my cabin. When the wind finally dies down we can always make our way to my place."

Brian did not look reassured a little while later when Marian tied an apron around his waist. "What's this for?"

"For the mess you're going to make."

"Me? I thought I was only going to help you?"

"And just how did you think you were going to help me?"

"Well, you know. You bake and I eat."

Marian laughed and kissed him on the cheek.

Brian pulled her into his arms and kissed her on the lips like he had wanted to do since lunch. Marian put her arms around his neck and kissed him back. She was going to miss this man when the roads cleared and she had to go back to her own cabin.

Brian released her slowly. "Okay, Miss Cookie Master. What do I do first?"

Marian still had her arms around his neck and said, "Kiss me again."

Brian kissed her again and again and again. Finally, he pulled away from her and said, "Marian if we don't start on those cookies now…"

Marian smiled and moved away from him. "Okay. You read the cookbook and I'll mix the ingredients."

Brian smiled. Now that he could do. "Sounds good. I read and then eat."

Marian laughed and began following his directions. When the dough was ready she portioned it off and rolled some out. She did not have cookie cutters for Christmas so she improvised and used a paring knife and small glass.

Brian watched in wonder as she made a snowman, Christmas tree, and what looked like a horse. A horse?

"Marian, uh…that looks like a horse."

"Brian, use your imagination, it's a reindeer."

Marian put the first batch in the oven and began to cut the other cookies into shapes. "Okay Brian, you cut some shapes too."

"Me? Shapes?"

Marian laughed. "It's easy. Here look." She took a glass, turned it over and made a circle. She then took the knife and shaped the outer edge to what looked like leaves. "See this is a Christmas reef."

Brian looked at her work and shook his head. "I'll decorate them and eat them."

Marian laughed and pulled the first batch from the oven to cool. She put more cookies on another cookie sheet and placed them in the oven. "Okay, these will be cool enough to decorate in a few minutes."

Brian reached for one and she slapped his hand. "No eating until they are decorated."

Marian found what she needed to make icing for the cookies and handed the bowl to Brian. "Decorate then eat."

Brian took the bowl and looked at the color. "But this is just white? What about the other colors?"

Marian went back into the pantry and found some cookie coloring and sprinkles. "Okay let me have the bowl." She separated the large bowl of icing into three different bowls and made one red, another one green and the other one she left white. "How is this?"

Brian smiled. "Now that is Christmas colors."

Marian brought the cooled cookies to the table and the bowls of icing. "Okay, Mr. Decorator. They are all yours. To decorate not eat."

"But you said I could eat them."

"Yes, but not all of them. Save some for me."

Brian frowned and Marian laughed.

Brain decorated the cookies while Marian cut them into shapes and baked them.

She would check his decorating and make sure he was not eating them. She laughed when she caught him with his mouth full of cookie.

"It was a defect." He said and then laughed.

They had a lot of fun cooking and decorating the cookies. Brian had eaten at least a dozen or more before they were through.

Marian shook her head. "I don't know where you put all those cookies."

Brian smiled and patted his stomach. "Right here."

They made three dozen cookies but Marian only managed to save a dozen and a half for the next day.

When the kitchen was cleaned up Brian said, "Let's check on the weather."

The storm was still raging on outside and the weather report said that it would not end until the next evening. There was another front coming in keeping this storm in the area longer than expected. Brian and Marian did not mind. It meant that they would have more time together.

Fate Is Surprising

While Marian was in the bathroom getting ready for bed Brian pulled out the sofa bed and arranged the pillows and blankets. Marian came out of the bathroom and saw the sofa bed already made up and smiled. Brian kissed her as he passed on his way to the bathroom to get ready for bed.

Marian lay on the sofa bed on her side and smiled. Today was fun. She laughed when she thought of making the cookies with Brian and all the cookies he ate. She wondered how he could be tired with all that sugar in him.

Brian came out of the bathroom and smiled. He was going to give her a massage. He just hoped he did it right. He had never given anyone a massage before. He had had plenty of them so he would just concentrate on what they did and what Marian did the night before.

Marian watched him approach the bed and noticed the smile on his face. He was up to something. "What are you up to?" She sat up and said, "You had too much sugar didn't you? You're not even tired."

Brian didn't say anything as he sat on the bed and lay down beside her. "Marian, you have a very suspicious mind." He pulled her down to him and kissed her.

Marian put her arms around his neck and kissed him back.

Brian pulled away from her and said, "Now lay on your stomach."

Marian asked, "Why?"

"Because I'm going to give you a massage like you gave me last night."

The thought of Brian's hands on her made her nervous. "Uh…I've…I'm not so sure…"

Brian frowned. "You don't want a massage?"

Marian shook her head. "Brian…I've…well, no one's ever given me a massage before. I mean…you know…like this. I've gone to a spa and had one but not like this."

Brian frowned then understood. His wife, Clara had never given him one either. "Well, that makes two of us. I have never had a massage by anyone other than at a spa or from the hospital staff."

Marian nodded and rolled onto her stomach. She closed her eyes and tried to relax.

Brian began with her shoulders and did what she had done to him the night before. He moved his fingers into her muscles softly like a caress and moved down her back. Marian began to relax and just let herself enjoy his hands on her back.

Brian was getting hot as he massaged Marian's back. He stopped and looked at her cute buttocks. He decided to skip that area and went to her thighs. He was careful not to get to high on her thighs as he massaged the muscles. He was surprised at how firm she felt in his hands but at the same time so soft. He wanted to do this without the barrier of her clothes on. Maybe later but not tonight.

He moved down her legs and massaged her calves and her feet.

When he was through, he kissed her on the neck.

Marian sighed and rolled over. "That was wonderful."

Brian smiled and kissed her and then he said what he was feeling. "I'd like to massage you like that without any clothes on."

Marian stared at him for so long that he thought he made a mistake. "I…" he swallowed and pulled away from her but Marian tightened her hold on his neck.

"Only if you let me do to same."

Brian smiled. "That is a deal."

Marian kissed him again then settled her head on his shoulder and put her arm across his waist. "Now go to sleep."

Brian didn't want to go to sleep. He wanted to kiss her again but she was right. They had time.

Fate Is Loving

The next day went like the one before. Brian worked on his laptop while Marian wrote more of her story.

After dinner Marian got out the cookbook and was looking for something else to make.

Brian looked over her shoulder as she stood at the counter. "What are we making tonight?"

Marian laughed. "You mean what am I making and you're eating?"

"That's what I said."

Marian shook her head and found a recipe for a Christmas reef. She wondered if they had the ingredients. She went to the pantry and Brian looked over the recipe and frowned. This looked hard.

Marian smiled and brought several things from the pantry. Then went back and brought out some more. The counter was full of the ingredients and Brian frowned at them. All this to make a cake?

Marian looked through the recipe again and checked the ingredients. "Are you ready?"

Brian frowned at the counter but shrugged his shoulder. "As ready as you are."

"Okay." Marian looked over the recipe again and placed three bowls on the counter. "Now you read the recipe like last night and I mix things together."

When it was ready, Marian placed the mixture in a pan, placed it in the oven, and set the timer. Then she washed the bowls and made the icing. "It has to set for a while before we can put the icing on it. So be patient."

Brian smiled and kissed her. "If you say so."

Marian laughed and kissed him back.

It would take about 45 minutes for the cake to bake so they played a couple of hands of poker. They used cookies for chips. Marian had to pat Brian's hand a few times when he tried to eat his winnings. "Brian, leave some room for the cake."

When the cake was done, Marian took it out of the oven and placed on the counter to cool. "Now according to the recipe, we shouldn't take it out of the pan for at least 30 minutes. Then we turn it over and put the icing on it."

Brian smelled the cake and didn't think he could wait 30 minutes. "Do we have to wait 30 minutes?"

Marian shook her head at him and said. "Yes."

Brian frowned and sat back down at the table. He snatched a cookie before she could stop him. "I'm practicing."

Marian laughed and dealt the cards.

Brian kept watching the clock and precisely 30 minutes later he stood up. "Okay icing time."

Marian went to the cake and put her hand on the side of the pan. It seemed to be cool enough. She put the knife around the edges and turned it over onto a plate. She tapped the bottom of the pan lightly with the handle of the knife and lifted the cake pan. She held her breath as she raised the pan.

Brian held his breath also. It smelled so good he did not care if it was not perfect. He was going to eat it anyway.

Marian smiled when only a small piece of the bottom of the cake stuck to the pan.

Brian reached for the icing but Marian stopped him. "Just a minute."

Brian looked on as Marian took the piece that stuck to the bottom of the pan and placed it perfectly back into place on the bottom of the cake. "Okay give me the bowl of icing."

Brian held the bowl close to him and said, "That's my job."

"Okay but be careful. Put the icing on the piece that came off first then spread it out evenly."

Brian did as he was told. He wanted to go faster but he knew that it was important to Marian that it looked good.

When he was finished he went to the cupboard and brought back two plates. Marian cut Brian a piece of cake and placed it on one of the plates. Brian looked at the small piece she cut for him and frowned. He picked it up in his hand and took a bite. He closed his eyes and savored the flavor.

Marian watched him and smiled when he put his plate down and took the whole cake to the table. Grabbing a fork on the way.

She laughed and followed him with the plate he set down on the counter. She pulled the cake from out in front of him and replaced it with the smaller piece on the plate. "Now Brian. You cannot eat the whole cake tonight."

Brian frowned at the small piece on the plate in front of him. "That is not fair. I worked hard making this cake and I want a bigger piece."

Marian sighed, cut him a larger piece, and added it to what he had on his plate. Brian smiled and began eating what was on his plate. Marian ate a piece of the cake and smiled. It was good.

Brian reached for more cake and Marian almost stopped him. She shook her head and only warned him. "Brian, sweetheart, you are going to make yourself sick if you don't slow down. You can have some more tomorrow."

Brian looked at the cake and realized that they had eaten half of it already. He put his fork down and leaned back in his chair. Then he thought of what she called him. Sweetheart. She'd called him sweetheart.

Marian filled his coffee cup and kissed him on the cheek. She sat back down across from him and noticed he was staring at her.

She put her hand over her mouth when she realized what she called him. She had never called a man 'sweetheart' before.

Brian smiled and got up from the table. He walked to her and pulled her up into his arms. "You called me 'sweetheart.'"

"I've...never called a man sweetheart before. Do you mind?"

"Not if I can call you 'sweetheart' also."

"No one has ever called me that before."

Brian searched her eyes for a moment before he kissed her. This was a woman made for loving and has had too little of it.

Marian and Brian cleaned up the kitchen and got ready for bed.

They lay in each other's arms for a long time before Brian asked. "Marian, sweetheart, can I…"

Marian smiled and looked at him. "Only if I can."

Brian kissed her and ran his hands over her. He put his hand on her breast and when she sighed, he held it more firmly. He deepened the kiss and rolled her onto her back. He let his hand move down her top and lifted it to feel her soft stomach. She had the softest skin. His hand moved upward and he caressed one breast and then the other. He kissed her neck then chin and moved to kiss her cheek.

Marian moved her hand under his pajama top, caressed his stomach, and moved her hand up to his chest. He had fine chest hair and she moved her hand around feeling it and caressed his nipple.

Brian moaned and brought his lips back to hers in a hungry kiss. He wanted to make love to her more than he had wanted anything in his life.

Marian was floating. She had never felt like this before. There was no fear when he touched or kissed her and she wanted more. She wanted to feel all of him. She began lifting his pajama top up his chest to take it off. She wanted to feel him next to her.

Brian pulled away from Marian and looked into her eyes. "Marian, are you sure?"

No, she was not sure but she wanted to find out. "I'm sure."

Brian kissed her softly, removed his pajama top, and reached for hers. She let him take it off and he pulled her to him.

It felt so wonderful to feel him next to her without any barriers between them. She wanted more time to hold him but he began to move his hands over her and he kissed her neck, and then took her breast in his mouth. He sucked gently at first then harder.

Marian could feel the panic rising in her and pushed on his shoulder.

Brian was hungry for her and did not realize she was pushing him away. He moved over her and kissed her deeply with a hungry passion he did not know he had.

Marian tried to control her fear and kissed him back. The panic grew again as he moved his hand lower and felt between her legs. She moved her hips to move his hand away and Brian thought she wanted more. Marian jerked her mouth from his and hit him on the shoulder as hard as she could. Brian stopped and stared at her. He rolled off her and tried to control his breathing. What happened? Did he do something wrong? Was he too rough?

Marian sat up and turned away from him. She lowered her head and began to cry. The tears came running down her face and she ran to the bathroom.

Brian sat up and watched her run away. He thought of following her but remained on the bed. He played back everything in his mind but he could not figure out what he did wrong. He asked her and she said she was sure. She liked his caresses.

She kissed him back. Then he frowned. She did push on his shoulder once but then stopped when he kissed her. Was she trying to tell him something then?

Brian hit the mattress with his fist. Why didn't she say something? Why did she let him go further? It was like with Clara all over again. He was just no good at this.

Marian wiped the tears from her eyes and knew she had to explain to Brian what happened. It was not him. She wanted him. It was the old fear that would not leave. She had to explain.

Marian walked back into the living room. Brian was gone. She looked in the kitchen but he was not there. She found him in his bedroom lying on the bed.

"Brian..."

"No, don't say it. Just go back to bed. I should have slept in here the whole time anyway."

Marian turned to go back to the living room but turned back to face him. "No. I need to explain what happened."

"No need. I was never good at…well, there's no need to explain."

Marian moved closer to his bed. "Please listen to me Brian, it wasn't you. It's me. I…" Marian sat on the edge of the bed.

Brian sat up and leaned against the headboard. He didn't say anything. He knew there was something she needed to say. How could she think there was anything wrong with her?

"I was walking home from school when I was twelve and a car pulled up beside me. He asked if I wanted a ride. I said no then he said he knew my father."

Brian knew what was coming but said nothing.

Marian wiped another tear from her cheek before she continued. "He didn't take me home. We ended up in the woods somewhere. I don't remember what happened but I feel I know what happened." She shook her head. "I don't know how I got home or anything. I knew my dress was dirty and threw it away."

Marian took a deep breath before continuing. "My mother wasn't the kind of person you could talk to so I said nothing. Actually, there was nothing to say because I didn't remember anything."

"I always wondered why I was not very good at love making. I've gone years without it and never minded." She gave a short laugh. "My sisters think I am crazy. They can't go a month without it and I go without it for years."

Marian got off the bed and faced Brian. "I didn't even remember the incident until four years ago. One night I had a dream and I knew somehow that it wasn't just a dream. Then, all those years of not wanting to be touched made sense. But I also realized that I have never had a man make love to me before either. They took what they wanted and rolled over and went to sleep."

She gave a short laugh again. "Do you realize I have written five novels that have excellent love scenes in them and they are all fantasy? All of them are from my imagination?"

She paused before continuing. "I'm sorry Brian. I wanted you so much I thought I…could please you. I've never really wanted to love a man before and I so much wanted to love you."

Marian started crying again and ran to the sofa bed in the living room. She threw herself onto the bed and buried her head in the pillow.

Brian sat on the bed for a while thinking of what she had said. It was not him. If he knew before what had happened to her he would have gone slower. She wanted to love him. No one had said that to him before.

Brian walked to the living room and sat on the side of the sofa bed. He put his hand on Marian's shoulder.

Marian felt Brian's hand on her shoulder and looked at him. Her eyes were red from crying. "Brian, I…"

Brian shook his head and moved her over so that he could lie down next to her. He pulled her into his arms and kissed the side of her head. "Go to sleep sweetheart. It's going to be all right."

Marian buried her face into his neck and held him close. She wanted to love him so much it hurt. "Brian."

Brian put his hand beneath her chin and raised her face to his. "We'll talk tomorrow. It's alright." He kissed her softly on the lips and put her head back on his shoulder. He fell asleep holding her and felt it was where he belonged.

Marian woke the next morning in Brian's arms. She lay still for a moment remembering the night before and moved away from him. How could he hold her like this after last night?

Brian felt Marian move away from him and he tightened his hold. Then he remembered her fear and let her go. He opened his eyes and put his hand on her arm. "Marian, sweetheart."

Marian stared at Brian but didn't move away.

Brian smiled at her and pulled her gently back into his arms. "It's alright sweetheart. Just let me hold you."

Marian put her head on his shoulder and put her arm across his waist. She wanted so much to love him.

Fate Is Understanding

Brian held her for a long time before he moved his right hand to her shoulder then caressed her gently from her shoulder to her hip and back again. He let his hand graze her breast on his way up and down from her shoulder to her hip. He could feel her response each time he touched near her breast.

Marian snuggled closer to Brian and let him touch her. It felt good. She moved her arm from his waist and started to touch him in the same way. She loved the feel of him.

Marian raised her head and kissed him on the lips and Brian kissed her back. He knew now to go slow so he would not frighten her again.

Marian smiled at him and he knew he loved her. He would control his passion and let her get used to him. He rolled onto his back and let her touch him. He moved his left hand to caress her shoulder and down her arm while his right hand moved over her neck and the tops of her breasts. He moved his hands gently and slowly.

Marian moved her hand over Brian's chest and stomach, caressing him as he was caressing her. She would kiss him on the cheek or his lips and pull away to kiss him on his chest, nipple, and stomach.

Brian was hurting. He wanted her so badly that if her hand went lower he would have to leave the bed.

Marian laid her head on his chest and listened to his rapid heartbeat. She knew what he wanted, needed, but was not sure she would not panic again. She looked up into his eyes and saw his hunger for her. She smiled at him and kissed him on the lips.

"Brian…it would be okay if you want to…" She did not finish but put her hand on his erection.

Brian pulled her hand away and shook his head. "I'm not like that my love. I want you there with me not just taking what you have to offer."

Marian kissed him again but his time it was different. She kissed him because she loved him. Brian felt the difference in her kiss and kissed her back. This special, kind, wonderful woman wanted him and he would go as slow as he needed even if it killed him. Marian ended the kiss and left the bed.

Brian watched her leave the bed and thought of the cold shower that awaited him. He put his arm over his eyes and sighed. It was going to be hell holding her and not make love to her, but if he could make it through what he had this past two years he could make it through the next few days. Maybe.

Brian shook his head and got up to fix the coffee. His mood improved when he saw the cake on the counter. Well at least he would die with a full stomach. She was definitely a great cook.

Marian smelled the coffee when she walked down the hallway to the kitchen. She knew she should feel embarrassed about what she had said to Brian last night but it felt good to tell someone.

Brian looked up and smiled when he saw Marian.

Marian looked at the half-eaten piece of cake on the plate in front of Brian and put her hands on her hips. "Brian. That was dessert for tonight."

Brian shook his head, "Nope. It's breakfast. We can make something else tonight."

Marian shook her head and headed for the coffee. She had created a monster.

She reached for the coffee and stopped when she realized the wind had stopped. She looked out the kitchen window and saw snow but no wind. She turned to Brian. "The wind has stopped."

Brian nodded. "While you were in the bathroom, I listened to the radio. They said the storm has passed and it should only be a few days before the roads are clear."

Marian poured a cup of coffee and sat down at the table. "You know I never asked how long you were staying up here."

"Through the New Year. And you?"

"Through the New Year."

Brian smiled. They had some time.

Marian smiled. They had some time.

"You know even when they clear the roads I want you to stay with me."

Marian stared at Brian for a moment before saying. "Even after last night?"

Brian nodded. "Last night was last night and this morning is this morning."

Marian smiled and nodded. She knew what he meant. It was nice this morning and every morning with him. She did not panic this morning when he touched her.

Brian picked up his fork and was about the take another bite of cake when the plate disappeared. He looked at Marian and frowned.

"Not for breakfast."

Brian watched Marian take his cake to the counter and wondered if he had made the right decision. They had to draw the line somewhere. Taking away a man's piece of cake was not allowed.

Brian changed his mind when Marian came back to the table and kissed him as she had earlier. Oh, well, there was always dessert tonight. Brian watched Marian fix breakfast and thought of the two desserts he was going to have after dinner.

Brian touched Marian as often as he could all day. A touch on the arm, his hand on her back, he held her hand, and he kissed the back of her hand once, he kissed her on the cheek, forehead, and neck and of course on those lovely lips of hers.

Marian was feeling so cherished by the end of the day she was putty in his hands that night. She lay in his arms, he touched her and kissed her, and there was no fear of him at all.

They both lay together without their pajama tops on, skin to skin and it felt wonderful. Brian did not let Marian's roaming hand go lower than the waistband on his pajamas and he did not caress her lower than her waistband.

He had to smile when she became frustrated because each time her hand would try to go further than his waist, he would kiss her hand and place it back on his chest.

Marian would take his hand and want to move it below her waistband and he would return it to her breast or neck.

Finally, Marian sat up and lay on top of him. She placed her hands on either side of his face and growled. "Look here buster, are you going to make love to me or not?"

Brian smiled at her and said, "My love, I am making love to you."

Marian stared at him and put her forehead on his. "I'm not used to…I…"

Brian placed his hands on either side of her face and brought her lips to his for a hungry, passionate kiss.

Marian could feel his hunger and kissed him with a hunger she had never known. So, this was making love. The touching, caressing, kissing, holding, and being together.

She had never known this before. It had always been so fast and then they rolled away.

Brian ended the kiss and laid her next to him. He rose up on an elbow and looked at her in the firelight. She was beautiful. He caressed her neck, breasts and stomach then lowered his mouth to her breast.

He ran his tongue around her nipple slowly and then moved to the other breast. Marian was so sensitive that she could not stand it. When he took her breast in his mouth she came off the bed. She grabbed his head and held it to her breast in fear that he would stop.

Brian sucked gently on one breast then the other. He knew he was torturing her but if he had to suffer then she would also. He wanted her to be ready for him. He would not frighten her again.

He moved his hand below her waistband and caressed the skin above it for a few minutes before he moved his hand lower. He still did not go under the material but touched her and caressed her through the material.

Marian rose off the bed to meet his hand.

Brian smiled and took his mouth from her breast and kissed her as his hand pressed harder between her legs.

Marian was going crazy. He was making her feel things she had never felt before. She moved her hand to touch him as he was touching her and he would again remove her hand. "Brian…" she panted. "Let…me…touch you."

Brian removed his hand from below her waist and placed her hand on him. "I want you Marian. Don't doubt that. But I don't want you frightened of me again."

Marian stared into his eyes and knew she would not be frightened of him. She kissed him and rolled him on his back where she lay on top of him.

She laid her head on his chest and took a deep breath. She lay there for a long while as Brian caressed her back and kissed the top of her head.

She felt…loved, cherished, and wonderful. Marian smiled and put her hands flat on his chest and rested her chin on them to look at him.

Brian looked into Marian's eyes and he could see love. Something he had never seen when a woman looked at him. He wanted it forever.

"Brian." Marian said his name softly.

"Yes, my love?"

"How long are you going to…love me before you make love to me?"

Brian smiled. "Until I feel you won't be frightened of me."

Marian frowned. "And when will that be?"

Brian thought for a moment then answered. "When I can have cake for breakfast."

Marian pushed on his chest and sat up. "Well, I never." Marian looked back at him and smiled but it was a very devious smile.

Brian saw that look and wondered what she was up to when she left the bed. He smiled when he saw her bringing what was left of the cake back to bed.

Brian sat up in anticipation. He could have more cake. She had only let him have a small piece after dinner.

Marian went around to his side of the bed and set the plate on his lap.

Brian smiled at her and looked at the cake but then he frowned when she took some of the frosting off the cake with her fingers and started smearing it on his chest.

"Marian…" Brian gasped in surprise.

"You said you wanted cake didn't you?"

Brian laughed and took some of the frosting in his fingers and caressed her breasts with frosting.

Marian put the plate of cake on the floor next to the bed and started licking the icing off his chest. Brian groaned and pushed her down on the bed and started licking and sucking the frosting from her breasts.

Marian twisted and was licking and sucking on his chest as he was sucking on her nipples and licking the icing off from her breasts.

Brian could not stand it any long and pulled off her pajama bottoms and then his. He lay on top of her and kissed her with a passion he had never known before. If she was afraid of him he was too far gone to even notice it. He had to have her.

Marian wanted him so badly no fear crept into her mind or body. All she knew was that she loved this man and needed him like her next breath.

Brian kissed her as his hand moved between them to caress her and feel her wetness. He knew she was ready and the innate instinct for mating took over and he could not control himself anymore.

He entered her quickly and heard her gasp. He kissed her and held himself still within her for a few moments before the need to move was so powerful he could not control it.

Marian held onto Brian and returned his kiss. The fear never came but there was some pain since it had been a long time for her. As she kissed him and caressed his back, the feeling she had earlier was returning and she started to move when he did. She met him thrust for thrust and could feel the pressure building.

She had never felt pressure like this before. It was growing stronger and was almost painful in its intensity and then she felt its release. She opened her mouth and groaned at the explosion to her senses.

Her body could not handle the shock waves of its force. The feeling was so foreign to her that she tried to get away from it.

Brian felt her climax and kissed her hard to keep her with him. He thrust one more time hard and found release himself.

Marian held onto Brian with all her might. She was crying from all the emotions, feelings, and passion she felt.

Brian lay on top of Marian, resting on his elbows and breathing hard. He put his forehead on hers for a moment then rolled to his side taking her with him. He held her in his arms and caressed her back. He had never felt anything like that before.

He did not realize Marian was crying until his breathing slowed enough for him to hear anything outside his own rapid breathing and heartbeat. He pulled back a little and put his hand under her chin to raise her face to his. "Marian, sweetheart. Did I hurt you?"

Marian was still crying but shook her head. "It…it was…" She could not finish and put her face in his neck and cried harder.

Brian did not know what to do so he held her. Did he frighten her? Hurt her? She said he did not hurt her so he just held her. He took it as a good sign when she lay in his arms and did not pull away. Finally, Brian reached for a tissue from the box on the table by the bed. He put his hand under her chin and raised her head so that he could dry her eyes and she could blow her nose.

Marian could not stop crying. She blew her nose in the tissue and could feel Brian wiping the tears from her eyes. She looked at his neck and saw that it was wet from her tears and cried even harder.

Brian was at a loss but he grabbed more tissue from the table and wiped her tears again and wiped his neck.

He pulled her back to him to hold her and after a long while she finally stopped crying and only sniffles were left in her.

Brian caressed her back and murmured comforting words to her all the while she had been crying.

Marian pulled away from him and felt something sticky on her chest. She looked down and saw the icing and then looked at his chest and started to laugh.

Brian frowned at her for a moment then looked at her chest and his and started to laugh also. He had forgotten about the icing.

They needed a shower. Brian pulled her up with him and walked her to the bathroom. He was going to leave her to shower on her own but she put her hand on his arm and pulled him into the shower with her.

Brian lathered the rag and washed her chest taking care to caress her breasts softly. Marian could stand it no more, took the rag from him, and caressed him as he had her. He moaned and pulled her into his arms and kissed her with the same hunger he had before.

They finally washed all the icing off, toweled each other dry before going back to the living room, and looked at the sheets. Icing was all over the sheets. They looked at each other and laughed.

Brian went to the hall closet for more sheets while Marian took the icing sheets from the bed. After the bed was made, in clean sheets, they lay down together and Brian held her close.

Brian held her for a long time before he asked, "Marian, sweetheart, why were you crying? Did I hurt you or frighten you?"

Marian shook her head. "That was the first time I have ever felt like that."

Brian knew it was fanciful and he never considered himself egotistical but at that moment, he felt more like a man than ever before. He brought her the pleasure no other man had been able to bring her.

Marian was silent for a while before she asked. She had to ask. "Brian, my love, was I…was it alright for you?"

Brian hugged her tight then released her a little. "It has never been like that for me my love. You were perfect."

Marian smiled and snuggled deeper in his arms. This is where she belonged.

Fate Is Caring

When they woke in the morning, they were still holding each other. Marian woke with a smile and Brian groaned. Marian looked over at him and wondered what was wrong.

Marian sat up and asked, "What's wrong?"

Brian could not move. The pain in his lower back was too great. "My…my back."

Marian rolled him onto his stomach and placed her hand on his lower back. She felt him and could feel the muscles were tense in the lower back area. "Hold on my love." Marian left the bed but did not know if he had a heating pad so she took some kitchen towels and let the hot water run over them. She took them back to the bed and placed one on his lower back and one above it.

Brian sighed as the warmth began to seep into his strained muscles.

"Brian, do you have a heating pad?"

Brian nodded. "Hallway."

Marian ran to the hallway and found the heating pad. She looked for an outlet but could not find one near the sofa bed. She looked at the fire and put another log on to build up the heat. Then she went into the bathroom and filled the tub with hot water. She checked it to make sure it was not too hot and went back for Brian.

She hoped he could walk to the bathroom. "Brian, sweetheart, we need to get you to the bathroom. Can you walk?"

Brian rolled over and sat up slowly. The pain in his lower back had eased but was still painful. He tried to stand, groaned, and sat back down. Marian put her hand on his arm and when he tried to stand again she helped pull him up.

Brian stood still for a while before he could walk to the bathroom. He walked slowly and stopped often.

Marian eased him down in the tub of hot water and knelt on the floor next to him.

She did not know what else to do except bring him some Tylenol. She raced to the kitchen and brought back the Tylenol and a glass of water.

Brian took the tablets and drank the water. He leaned back in the hot water and sighed. Marian sat on the floor next to him and waited. Brian closed his eyes and laid his head back on the tile relaxing his body as much as he could. The hot water felt good and the Tylenol should kick in anytime now.

Marian checked the water often to make sure it was still warm for him. She felt it cooling, pulled the drain, and let more hot water run into the tub.

After thirty minutes, the pain started to ease and he opened his eyes.

Marian smiled and said, "You are a powerful lover sweetheart, I guess I'll have to take it easy on you next time."

Brian laughed lightly and said, "Not a chance my love. You just give me a little time and I'll be right back in there."

Marian smiled. "Well, since you seem to be doing better, I'll go make the coffee and fix breakfast this morning. Do not try to get out of this tub without me. I'll be right back."

Brian nodded and closed his eyes.

Marian checked the water and was satisfied that it was warm enough and left to fix the coffee. She washed her face in the kitchen sink, put on her pajamas, and made the sofa bed back into a couch.

Brian was sitting up in the water when she returned. He looked at her and frowned. "You covered up my view."

Marian shook her head and knelt by the tub. "I think you have had all you can stand for today."

Brian shook his head. "You just let me rest today and tonight I'll show you what this old man can do."

Marian laughed and helped him out of the tub. "Well, old man, if you insist on playing macho guy, I'll be on top tonight."

Brian kissed the top of her head and said, "Kinky."

Marian helped him dry off and put his pajamas back on. They were loose fitting. She did not want any pressure on those back muscles.

They walked slowly back to the living room and Marian helped him sit on the couch. "Now you sit here and I'll bring you some coffee and your breakfast."

"I am not an invalid Marian."

Marian knelt beside him and put her hand on his knees. "Sweetheart. Would you agree that your back hurts you this morning?"

Brian nodded reluctantly.

"And can we also agree that the extra activity from last night caused your back to hurt this morning?"

Brian nodded again.

"Therefore can we concede that since I was a party to the extra activity that caused your back to hurt that I have some responsibility in pampering you this morning?"

"Marian…"

Marian placed her hand on his lips to silence him. "Brian, you gave me something last night that was wonderful. Something I never expected. And I was going to fix breakfast this morning anyway."

Brian looked into Marian's eyes and smiled. "Okay, but only this morning. I will fix lunch."

Marian kissed him on the lips, put a blanket over his lap, and went into the kitchen to fix breakfast.

Brian sat on the couch and stared into the fire. He hated being like this but he had used the lower back muscles a lot of last night. He smiled when he thought of last night. He hurt this morning but it was worth it. The he frowned. Could he make love to her again tonight?

Marian turned on the radio and the announcer said it was Christmas Eve. Marian stopped what she was doing and looked at Brian sitting on the couch. Christmas Eve.

Tomorrow was Christmas. She looked around the cabin but did not see any Christmas decorations. No tree or garland. Nothing.

She looked in the pantry and found some popcorn. She had noticed that there was a sewing kit in one of the drawers in the kitchen. They could string some popcorn. She looked up on the top shelves and saw a box labeled Christmas. She reached for it but it was too high. She looked around, found a little stepladder, and climbed up to take the box down. She put the box on the floor and looked around again but could not see any other boxes labeled Christmas. She put the stepladder away, took the box into the living room, and set it on the couch next to Brian. He looked at the box and then back at Marian.

"It's Christmas Eve, Brian. See what we have in the box for Christmas decorations. I found some popcorn and string, so we can string some popcorn." Marian went back into the kitchen to finish breakfast.

Brian looked at the box again and then back at Marian. He did not have anything to give her for Christmas. He looked around the cabin and could not think of anything he had that she would appreciate. Women always liked jewelry and fine things.

He looked at the box and moved it closer. He opened it and started taking the Christmas items out. They did not have a tree and with the snow so deep outside and with his back like it was, they would not have one.

Marian watched Brian take the Christmas decorations out of the box and thought of what to give him for Christmas. She did not have anything at her cabin and they could not get to Mrs. Meghan's store for a few more days. She could give him another massage. Actually, she would give him one this afternoon. It should help his back. She could get him something later.

Marian brought Brian his breakfast, moved the Christmas decoration aside, and sat next to him on the couch. She looked at the decorations while they ate then looked around the cabin. Some ideas were forming in her mind.

She could keep Brian busy stringing popcorn while she decorated. She frowned when she thought of how to make a tree. She looked around again but did not see anything that would resemble a tree.

She put her plate down on the floor and looked out the window. Snow everywhere. There was no wind which was good. She opened the front door and found that it was half blocked with snow. She peered out and saw that the snow was too deep to go walking around in to look for a tree. She did not see a tree stand anywhere in the pantry. She peered over at the shed and saw that the door was almost completely covered with snow. She could move it away from the door to look inside but again there was the problem of cutting down a tree.

Marian closed the door and looked around the room again.

Brian noticed Marian was looking for something and asked, "What are you looking for?"

"A tree. The snow is too deep to go walking through looking for a tree and even if we did find one I don't know if we have a tree stand."

Brian thought for a moment and tried to stand. The pain in his lower back was only a slight discomfort now and he stretched to limber it. "Hand me my canes."

Marian retrieved his canes and handed them to him.

Brian took the canes and took a few steps. He smiled and took a few more. "Okay. I think there is a tree stand in the shed. My son's came up here for Christmas a couple of years ago and I know they had a tree. As for cutting a tree let's look around and see if we can find one."

"Brian the snow is too deep."

Brian shook his head. "Maybe not. Let's at least try."

Marian nodded and went into the bathroom to get dressed.

Brian walked to his bedroom and put on his warmest clothes.

Brian met Marian by the door and they cleared the snow away from the doorway and stepped out onto the porch. Brian looked around the yard and moved forward clearing a path as he went.

He went down the steps and began walking towards the shed. Marian followed behind him ready to catch him if he fell.

They reached the shed and began moving the snow away from the door. Marian wished she had a shovel.

Brian opened the door to the shed and walked to the far corner. There was a pile of boxes covered with a tarp. He removed the tarp and Marian helped him look through the boxes. They found a tree stand and Marian took it back to the cabin.

Brian looked around the yard and remembered they had found a tree a few yards to the north of the cabin a couple of years ago. He dropped one of his canes and picked up the axe.

Marian returned to the shed, saw Brian with the axe in one hand, and frowned. "Brian, the snow is too deep."

Brian shook his head and started making a path through the snow. A few yards from the cabin he stopped. The pain in his back was coming back. He took a deep breath and continued walking.

Marian knew he was in pain but said nothing. She just followed him and was ready to catch him or help him if he needed it.

Brian stopped about fifty yards from the cabin and pointed to a small pine tree. "How about that one?"

Marian looked at the small tree and looked around at the other trees in the area. She saw one that she liked better. It was larger and fuller. She pointed to it and said, "I like that one."

Brian looked at the tree and nodded. He walked over to it and put down his cane. Marian held her breath as he raised the axe to cut down the tree.

Brian raised the axe and let go of the first swing at the tree trunk. His back hurt but not too bad. He hit the tree again and again until it fell. He put down the axe and leaned on the handle for a moment before bending down to pick up the cut end of the tree.

Marian rushed forward and said, "That's my job. You cut it down and I get to drag it back to the house."

Brian stood and retrieved his cane.

Marian pulled the tree back to the cabin and up the steps. Brian followed. As soon as he was inside the cabin, he headed for the couch and sat down heavily.

Marian put the tree just inside the door and looked at the tree stand.

Brian laid his head back and closed his eyes. He opened them when he felt someone put some tablets in his hand.

"Here," Marian said, "Take some of these."

Brian nodded and took the tablets and the glass of water.

Marian brought a pillow from the bedroom and put it on the couch. She then removed his boots and coat, laid him down on the couch, and covered him with a blanket. "Now you rest. You did your job, I'll do mine."

Brian nodded and closed his eyes. He was asleep almost immediately.

Marian smiled at him and looked over at the tree. She should have been satisfied with the littler one. She struggled with the tree for an hour before she got it in the stand and found a place to put it.

She looked at the box of decorations and started putting them on the tree. She would make up the popcorn later when Brian woke up.

Fate Is Generous

Brian slept through lunch and Marian was not going to wake him. She took the time to make some more Christmas cookies. She smiled when they came out of the oven. Maybe this time she could finish the batch without half of them disappearing.

Brian smelled the cookies and opened his eyes. Cookies. His mouth began to water and he sat up on the couch. His back felt a little stiff and only a little pain. He reached for his cane and stood slowly.

Marian looked over at Brian and frowned. What was he doing? He should be resting.

Brian walked slowly to the kitchen and sat at the table. "Icing." Was all he said and Marian laughed.

Every third cookie Brian put icing on he said, "Defect" and crammed it in his mouth.

Marian shook her head and laughed at him. She was glad he was feeling better.

After the cookies were finished and again, only half of what she made lasted through the icing phase, she made the popcorn for the tree.

Brian sat on the couch stringing popcorn while Marian put together a stew for dinner. She set it on the stove to cook and joined him on the couch.

She strung the string of popcorn on the tree and stepped back to look at what she had done. It looked pretty good.

Brian smiled. The tree was beautiful. Then he frowned when his stomach began to make noises. "Sweetheart, I'm hungry. Could you make me a sandwich?"

Marian stared at Brian for a moment before answering. "Hungry? Brian less than two hours ago you ate more than a dozen cookies."

"Defects." Brian said. "They were cookie defects. And that was just dessert. I need sustenance."

Marian laughed and went to the kitchen to fix him a sandwich. She fixed one for herself as well and they sat on the couch and ate in silence.

Brian finished his sandwich and said, "I don't have anything to give you for Christmas sweetheart. Can I give you something later?"

"Brian, you have given me the most precious gift there is. I don't need anything else."

Brian frowned. "What did I give you?"

Marian kissed him on the cheek. "You gave me you, my love."

Brian smiled and kissed her on the lips softly then pulled her into his arms and deepened the kiss.

Later that night as they lay in each other's arms Brian began to caress Marian and she pulled his hand away. "Not tonight. You need to rest."

Brian frowned. "Rest? I feel great." He started to caress her again and she stopped him again.

Brian rolled onto his back and sighed.

Marian rose up on an elbow and looked at him. "Sweetheart, you know I want to make love to you, but after this morning I would be worried that you would hurt yourself again."

Brian looked at her and said, "Okay. You mentioned kinky this morning. You can get on top."

Marian smiled and licked her lips. "Hmmm. Now that has promise." The thought of making love to him inspired all kinds of ideas. She noticed a bottle of baby oil in the bathroom. "I'll be right back." She would give him a massage then kiss him all over and then… Well kinky was kinky.

Brian watched her leave the bed and frowned. What was she going to do?

When she returned and he saw the bottle of baby oil in her hand he lifted and eyebrow. "Baby oil?"

"Now my love we are going to play a game. You are an invalid. I am your nurse. It is my job to relax you and make you happy."

Brian frowned for a moment then smiled. "Hmmm. I thought it was called playing doctor."

Marian laughed. "Strip and roll over patient sweetheart and I'll give you a massage."

Brian sat up, took off his top, and removed the bottoms then rolled onto his stomach.

Marian sat on the bed next to him and ran her hand over his back before putting some oil into her palms and rubbing them together to warm the oil. She massaged his back and then removed her pajamas and sat across his buttocks and massaged his lower back.

Brian moaned when he felt Marian on his buttocks.

Marian stopped rubbing his lower back when she heard him moan. "Am I hurting you?"

Brian shook his head.

Marian smiled and continued the massage. She moved down and tonight she massaged his buttocks before moving to massage his legs.

Brian was in heaven and hell. He loved the feel of her hands on him but his erection was pressing into the mattress and becoming very painful. "Sweetheart?"

"Yes?"

"Uh…I need to roll over."

"But I haven't done your legs yet."

"Sweetheart I seem to have a problem that needs to be taken care of."

Marian frowned for a moment them laughed. "You may roll over."

Brian sighed and rolled over.

Marian kissed his arousal and he almost came off the bed. She smiled and kissed it again and loved his response.

She put some baby oil on her hands and rubbed them together before caressing his shoulders, chest, stomach, and thighs. Brian moaned and grabbed for her. Marian moved away from his reach and continued her caressing. She kissed his nipple and licked it, then sucked on one then the other.

"Marian." Brian groaned.

Marian lay down on top of him and kissed him on the neck, cheek, and lips. Brian caught her head in his hands and held her to him while he kissed her. If she did not stop this torture, he would come too soon.

Marian moved out of his arms and straddled him. She placed herself over his erection and slowly moved back and forth.

Brian groaned again.

Marian leaned down and kissed each nipple then moved down further to taste him. She licked him, put her hand around him, and caressed him slowly.

"Marian." Brian groaned. "I can't…it's too much."

Marian moved back over him and took him inside her. She moved up and down and could feel the pressure building with each thrust.

Brian took her by the shoulders and leaned her towards him enough so that he could capture one of her nipples in his mouth. He could feel himself coming and tried to hold back but he could not. It was an incredible feeling when they both had the release at the same time. Marian called out and so did Brian.

Afterward Marian slumped down on Brian's chest and he wrapped his arms around her. They held each other and neither one could say anything for a long while.

Marian rolled off him onto her side and kissed him on the cheek. "Thank you, my love."

Brian turned his head to look at her and said, "Thank you. You make an excellent nurse."

Marian laughed and kissed him. She then looked at the oil on both of them and thought another shower was in order.

Brian caressed her breasts and could feel the baby oil. "We'll have to get some of the flavored oil."

Marian laughed and rolled off the bed. "In the meantime, we need another shower."

Brian sat up slowly and tested the pain in his back. There wasn't any and he smiled.

The next morning Marian woke and wondered if Brian's back would be hurting.

Brian woke and rolled onto his back.

Marian asked, "How does your back feel?"

Brian opened his eyes and felt his back. Nothing. It did not hurt. "It's okay. You really are a great nurse."

Marian smiled and kissed him on the cheek. "Merry Christmas darling."

Brian had always wanted to hear those words. "Merry Christmas to you my love."

Fate Is A Sweet Lady

Christmas Day passed and then another day and another. The roads were finally cleared and Marian could go back to her own cabin.

The man that knocked on their door to tell them the roads were cleared also told her that they had pulled her SUV from the ditch and had it towed into town. It should be ready in a day or so. There was minor damage to the front end.

Marian was silent during lunch and Brian knew something was wrong. "Marian, what's wrong?"

"The roads are clear. I…should be getting back to my own cabin."

Brian frowned. "Do you want to leave?"

Marian looked at him and said, "Well, no but…"

Brian stood and walked towards her. He took her shoulders and raised her to stand in front of him. "Tell me now Marian. Do you want to spend time with me, be with me?"

Marian could feel the tear running down her cheek. "Oh yes Brian."

Brian pulled her into his arms and held her. "Then we can either stay here or we can go to your cabin together."

Marian hugged him and laid her head on his chest. She did not know what would happen next week but she knew she wanted to be with him always.

Since the food supply was low, they went to her cabin. Brian packed his clothes and they drove to her cabin a few hours later. They spent the rest of their time together in her cabin and made love every morning and night.

The day had finally arrived for them to go back to their own lives.

Brian went back to his cabin to pack his things and Marian packed her clothes and put them in the SUV. She waited for Brian to come back. They had not talked about what they were going to do after they left.

Brian was thinking of what to do about Marian. He wanted her in his life but she had a life of her own. They did not even live in the same state. He had his business and commitments and the doctors' were talking about another operation. He was walking without using either cane but only for short distances. His back had not bothered him since that one night. He would go see the doctors when he got back and talk to them.

Marian was wondering what Brian would want to do. She had commitments and had established herself at the University and the department of Education in her state and his business was in another state. Everything she had worked for over the years was happening.

Brian pulled up in front of Marian's cabin and got out slowly. He knew they had to talk but they had each been putting it off.

Marian was sitting at the kitchen table waiting for him.

Brian sat down across from her and started by saying. "I have to talk to the doctors when I get back. They want to do another operation but maybe I don't need one. We both live in different states and each of us have commitments."

Marian nodded. "We could visit each other during the year and plan on meeting here next Christmas."

Brian did not like that but he agreed.

Throughout the next year, Brian and Marian met often for long weekends and twice for a week together. They emailed each other weekly and talked on the telephone as often as possible. The love was still there.

It was three weeks before Christmas and Marian was driving to her cabin when a deer ran out in front of her and she swerved to miss it. Her SUV went into a ravine and she was badly hurt. She was rushed to the hospital in critical condition. Her family was notified but no one else. She had not told her children about Brian.

Brian arrived at the cabin and waited for Marian. Two days he waited before he went to her cabin and found it empty. He went to see Mrs. Meghan but she had not seen her either. Brian knew something was wrong. The year they spent together was wonderful. The love they shared last year was still there.

He asked to use Mrs. Meghan's phone. He called her home and there was no answer. He called her cell phone and another woman answered. "I'd like to speak to Marian Carstairs please."

"Who's calling?" The woman asked.

"Brian Mason."

"I'm sorry, Mr. Mason, but my mother is in critical condition right now and can't talk to anyone."

Critical condition? "What happened? Where is she?" The panic in his voice must have gotten through to the young woman because she answered him.

"She is in a coma at St. Mary's hospital in Springfield."

"I'm on my way. Tell her I am coming."

"Mr. Mason…"

Brian's voice was firm when he said, "Tell her. I'll be there in less than two hours."

Karen looked at the phone for a moment then put it back to her ear. "Are you the man she spent Christmas with last year?"

"Yes."

Karen smiled. She had seen a difference in her mother this past year. "I'll tell her Mr. Mason."

Brian drove the two-hour drive to Springfield in record time. He parked his car and ran into the hospital. "Ms. Marian Carstairs, where is she?"

The nurse looked up the name and it said family only. "Are you a member of the family?"

Brian automatically said, "Yes." Then said, "No. We're friends."

The nurse shook her head. "I am sorry, Sir. Only family members can see her."

Brian cursed then remembered the woman he talked to on the cell phone. It might have been her daughter. "Can I speak to her daughter?"

The nurse looked doubtful but called the room. She spoke to someone and then hung up the phone. "Her daughter is on her way down."

Brian paced back and forth in the reception area waiting for someone to come.

Karen stopped and watched a man pace back and forth for a moment before approaching him. "Mr. Mason?"

Brian looked at the woman and nodded. This had to be Marian's daughter. She looked a lot like her. "Yes. How is she? Can I see her?"

"Yes, follow me."

Brian did not speak again until he was in the room and took hold of Marian's hand. "What happened? What do the doctor's say?"

"Her SUV ran off the road and into a trench. It tumbled down the hill into a ravine. She's lucky to be alive. She's been in a coma for three days. The doctors have done all the tests they can think of. She has a concussion and some bruises but that's all."

"No broken bones, no ruptures. They just don't know why she won't come out of the coma."

"How bad was the head injury?"

"Pretty bad but nothing that would cause permanent damage."

Brian pulled a chair up next to her bed and looked around. "Why doesn't she have a private room?"

"There wasn't any available."

"When will there be one available?"

Karen shook her head. "Not until another week."

Brian sat in the chair holding her hand and began to speak to her. "Marian, I'm here my love. Feel my hand in yours, listen to my voice. I need you. Please open your eyes and look at me."

Karen listened to the pleading passion in his speech and moved out into the hallway. This man loved her mother. She called her brothers and told them about Mr. Mason. She believed if anyone could bring her mother out of the coma he could.

Marian's sons and their wives visited often over the next few days but Brian never left her side. He ate at the hospital and slept in the chair resting his head on her bed. He talked to her constantly.

Three days after Brian arrived, Marian opened her eyes. Brian was asleep holding her hand and his head lay by her waist on the bed. Marian looked around the room and saw the IV running from her left hand. She picked it up slowly and put her hand on Brian's head.

Brian felt something on his head and opened his eyes. He raised his head and saw Marian's eyes were open. "Oh my God." He pushed the button for the nurse and kissed Marian on the cheek. "Hello my love. Welcome back."

Marian smiled as much as she could and closed her eyes again.

When the nurse came running into the room Brian told her Marian opened her eyes and moved her hand.

The nurse went quickly to find the doctor.

"Marian, sweetheart, open your eyes again. Look at me." Brian kissed the back of her hand he was still holding.

Marian opened her eyes and looked at him. "Brian, my love."

"Yes, my sweet. It's me. The doctor is on his way."

"Doctor? What happened?"

"You had an accident my love. You've been in a coma for almost five days."

"Five days?"

"It's all right my love. I'm not going to leave you."

Marian smiled. She was going to tell him that nothing mattered except him. She was going to live wherever he was so that they could be together more.

Brian had decided that nothing was more important than Marian and he was going to live wherever she was. He would run his company long distance if necessary.

Karen came into the room and watched her mother and Brian for a moment before she spoke. "Well Mother. Welcome back."

Marian looked at her daughter. "Hello Karen."

Karen began to cry and Brian moved aside as Karen approached her mother and gave her a hug.

Marian hugged her daughter and patted her head. "It's all right dear. I'm going to be fine. Brian will take care of me, won't you sweetheart?"

Brian nodded and asked, "You will marry me, won't you? It looks like taking care of you may be a full-time job."

Marian smiled and nodded.

"Karen, find a preacher before she changes her mind."

Karen hugged her mother then hugged Brian and left to make the arrangements.

Marian shook her head. "Brian, you can at least wait until I am out of this bed."

Brian shook his head. "No way."

Brian moved aside and Marian closed her mouth from comment when the doctor arrived.

The doctor looked at Marian and Brian and raised an eyebrow. "Ms. Carstairs, are you arguing with the man who would not leave your side for three days?"

Marian stared at Brian. "You have been here three days?"

"And nights." The doctor added.

"Oh. Brian." Marian said and started to cry.

Brian looked at the doctor. "Can't you do something?"

The doctor shrugged his shoulders. "Like what Mr. Mason? From all the tests we've run, she's fine. She just had to come out of her coma. There's a lot we know but we do depend on this time of year when we can. It is the time of year for miracles."

Brian held Marian's hand and agreed. This was the time of year for miracles.

Brian and Marian were married in the hospital chapel the next morning. Brian had called his sons and Karen had taken care of Marian's side of the family. It was a short ceremony as Marian was still recovering from her accident.

The doctors released Marian a week later and Brian took her to his cabin. He sat her on the couch with a pillow behind her head and covered her with a blanket. She frowned at him but he only shook his head. "You will stay put and be a good patient."

Marian smiled and asked, "Does this mean that you are the nurse this time?"

Brian tried to be stern but he laughed. "You are a kinky woman, Mrs. Mason."

"That's what you love about me my sweet." Marian batted her eyelashes for effect.

Brian laughed and fixed her a cup of coffee. When he returned with coffee for them both, he was determined to get it straight where they were going to live.

"Now Marian, my love. You have commitments and I have commitments. We live in different states. We need to decide where we're going to live."

"Well, I can teach anywhere. I have my PhD you know. I can apply at the University and get involved in education in your state. And don't forget, I can write my novels anywhere."

"But would you be happy there?"

"Sweetheart, this past year of not being with you every day was terrible. I want to be with you wherever you are."

"I can run my business from home and that means I can live anywhere."

Marian sighed. "All right, where is the map?"

Brian found a map in his bedroom and put it her lap. Marian opened the map and spread it out. "All right. We both agree that we can live anywhere we choose. I can teach online classes and teach anywhere. I have enough money that I don't have to work and you can work from home. So, where would you like to live?"

Brian looked at the map and looked around the cabin. "Actually, I wouldn't mind living here all year round."

Marian frowned. "But there's no internet or cell phone service up here."

"I know, so that's out of the question. But I do like living in this area."

Marian looked at the map and saw a town about two hours from their cabins. "Look at this little town. What do you think about living there? We can take a look next week and see if it's what we want."

Brian agreed and kissed her on the cheek. "Now get some rest."

They traveled to the little town the next week and they loved it. Marian inquired about teaching and there was a branch of the state University there that would love to have her teach some classes. There was internet service available and they found the perfect house. They could each have their own workroom plus enough bedrooms for the children to visit.

The next Christmas they invited all of their children to spend the holidays with them and it was a house full. Everyone got a long fine.

Brian and Marian walked in their garden after dinner on Christmas Eve and looked at the stars. They both had what they had always dreamed of. Christmas was truly a time for miracles.